Death in the Dune

by
John Molino

Best Wishes.
John Molino
Nov'19

ISBN 9781698876498

For my grandchildren
Bella, Alana, Marshall, Carter, & Sean
&
their parents
Bill & Anna
Chris & Heather
Matt & Jennie

Maybe this world is another planet's hell.

Aldous Huxley

Cape Henry, the Virginia Settlement
June 1617

Jonathan Spires was gone. The twelve-year old was talked about as "missing" for nearly a week, before it was generally accepted that he was, in fact, gone.

Sara, his mother, held onto the hope that he would walk through the door of their cabin that day and every day thereafter. Charles Spires feared the worst from the moment his wife voiced concern about Jonathan's tardiness.

The Nansemond were understandably suspicious of the larger motives that brought foreigners to their shore. It was tense when the English first came ashore at Cape Henry. A month after their initial landing, the majority of the settlers sailed up river to establish Jamestown. Those few families remaining at the original landing site soon made peace with the natives. Since then, the English settlers and the indigenous Nansemond people of the Tidewater Virginia region had been living together harmoniously for nearly a decade.

No one suspected Nansemond involvement in Jonathan's disappearance. In fact, all of Jonathan's closest friends were boys within a year or two of his age from the tribe. The other English boys didn't seem to have Jonathan's thirst for adventure. He liked the Nansemond and they liked him. Jonathan helped them with rudimentary English, and, thanks to these friends, Jonathan picked up a great deal of their Algonquin-rooted language.

When Jonathan was late for dinner that June night, his parents assumed the twelve-year old was off with his friends and had again lost track of time. In fact, the boys had spent most of the day exploring a bit of land close to where the Chesapeake Bay met Broad Bay. When Charles and some men from the settlement stopped at the reservation, they learned Jonathan's friends came home well before dinner.

Several Nansemond men joined Charles and his English companions to walk the route Jonathan was almost certain to have taken. They found nothing.

When Elvy, the Nansemond medicine woman, heard that Jonathan was missing, she left her home to be with Sara. Elvy had treated Jonathan when the Spires arrived at Cape Henry from England. That was three years ago. He had developed a fever the last few days of their journey. Jonathan had been so weak that Charles carried him from the ship.

The settlement's English doctor concluded Jonathan would die, but accepted Elvy's offer to help at the urging of Sara and Charles, who were desperate. They rightly credited Elvy with saving Jonathan's life. Since then, Elvy was respected throughout the settlement. Elvy helped Sara throughout her pregnancy with Dori, Jonathan's one-year-old sister.

Elvy had become almost a sister to Sara. Elvy wasn't her Nansemond name. Sara began to call her Elvy, which was as close as she could come to pronouncing her actual name. It stuck. The entire settlement now called her Elvy.

Later that night, the Nansemond Chief called for Jonathan's two closest friends from the tribe and their fathers. Using the light of the full moon, the five of them retraced the route the search party had covered earlier in the evening.

"What we are about to do," the Chief told them, "will not be spoken of to anyone at anytime for any reason. Is that clear?" He made each of them acknowledge his directive and swear with their lives they would obey.

The Chief was unarmed, but suspended from a belt around his waist was a rolled piece of stitched animal skin. The others recognized it as the Nansemond equivalent of a sleeping bag—a child's sleeping bag. The Chief offered no explanation for why he had it. Neither the boys nor their fathers asked.

Each father was armed with a knife, a bow, and a quiver containing a few arrows. The boys each had a sheathed knife. When their search came to the beachfront of the Chesapeake Bay, the Chief stopped and spoke privately with the boys. He then motioned for the parents to join them. They continued along the beach only a short distance more when the Chief stopped a second time.

He instructed them to be quiet. He moved to the edge of the dune, looked upward, and stretched both arms to the sky. His perspiration-soaked arms appeared to be rods of light as they reflected the moonlight. After no more than a minute, he slowly lowered his arms until they extended over the dune.

The Chief told the boys and their fathers to stay on guard where they were. He began to walk into the dune when one of the men begged him not to go in at all, or, at least, not alone.

"I will be fine. Oki has no use for old men. You stay here. The boys have told me this is the right location. Do not follow me. If I have not returned by sunrise, return home and begin the process to select a new Chief."

He proceeded slowly, but without hesitation, into the dune. Soon, he was out of sight.

After no more than fifteen minutes, one of the boys noticed movement of the tips of the dune grass. The men drew their bows. Whatever it was, it was coming toward them. Each boy held his breath and moved behind his father for protection.

It was the Chief. He was physically unharmed, but his face bore an unmistakable look of sadness.

He held the sleeping bag vertically in one hand. The Chief had pulled the laces tight and tied their ends, sealing it. It was obvious there was something inside the sleeping bag, yet there was no movement.

The boys feared the worst, but were encouraged when they saw the Chief. He offered no explanation and none of them questioned him. They assumed he had picked up a small animal. Based on the ease with which he carried the modestly sized bag, they didn't give a second thought to the possibility that it might contain Jonathan's remains.

The boys' fathers said nothing the entire walk back to the reservation. Words were not needed. They knew there was, in fact, one way Jonathan's remains could easily fit in the sleeping bag. Without saying it, they were relieved they had been instructed never to talk about what they had done that night.

When they arrived, the Chief reminded them of their oath. He urged them to get as much sleep as possible and told them to be prepared to join the search for Jonathan in the morning.

There was very little sleep in the English settlement that night. At first light, Charles and a larger group than the night before set out to retrace Jonathan's likely course. In addition to several Nansemond men, Jonathan's young friends joined the search, including the two boys and their fathers. As they worked their way back to Cape Henry, the Englishmen moved to the beach along the southern edge of the Chesapeake Bay. This was the most direct route to the settlement at Cape Henry. Charles knew Jonathan always used the beach when he walked home from this general area.

When several of the settlers suggested they expand into the dune, the Nansemond counseled against it.

"No good happens in the dune. The boys know," they advised Charles.

"I understand, but we have to look. We'll be very careful," Charles told them.

If Jonathan had been attacked by an animal, he might have been dragged into the dune. Charles would not allow an area to go unsearched solely because of a Nansemond legend.

They walked in pairs, thoroughly searching the beachfront and the dune until they came to Cape Henry, where the Bay meets the Atlantic Ocean.

When Charles walked into the cabin alone, carrying Jonathan's shoes and walking stick, Sara began to sob.

"Elvy. Oh, Elvy. Please stay the night with my baby. I have to find my son and bring him home," she begged between her tears.

Jonathan's mother began moving about the family cabin, preparing to go out on her own to search for Jonathan. Charles managed to change her mind, but only after he explained how many had been looking for Jonathan and the thoroughness of their search.

When he mentioned he had found the shoes in the dune, it was Elvy's turn to wail. She put her head in her hands and let out an unearthly groan. She rocked forward and back in her chair, her eyes firmly closed.

"Oki," she said. "Oki. No, no, no. Oki."

Charles and Sara had heard Elvy mention Oki to Jonathan. When he began going out on his own or with the other boys, Elvy warned him about the areas where wild animals were known to roam or where recent storms had washed out certain trails. She always ended with her general warning about the danger in the dune and the presence of Oki, the god who takes away good things. Charles and Sara assumed Oki (and the accompanying story) was more myth than fact. Here, in the presence of this woman they had come to respect so much, they realized the depth of her belief.

Oki was the last thing on Jonathan's mind as he moved along the familiar route leading to Cape Henry. He knew from the vegetation along the trail and the break in the trees that he was at the point where he routinely cut through to the beach along the Bay's shoreline. Jonathan followed his routine. He removed his shoes, tied the laces together, and hung the shoes over his shoulder. He loved walking barefoot on the beach.

He saw the ship on the horizon and wondered if it carried additional settlers from England. He would enjoy teaching young boys who might settle here about the Bay, the Nansemond, and life in the Tidewater. But, there was something unusual about this ship.

With its sails down, clearly at anchor, the ship was much farther out than any of the other vessels that arrived since he and his family began living at the Cape Henry settlement. There were no signs of activity on board the ship, but, of course, it was a good distance away.

Jonathan wasn't sure what lured him into the dune. Although it wouldn't be the first time he ignored his mother's admonitions about coming straight home, he had never before wandered into the dune alone.

Elvy's warnings were stories meant only to scare a little kid, he told himself. *And besides, I've never seen a dangerous, wild animal near here. Never even had a close call.*

Jonathan decided to go fairly deep into the dune and then turn to the east, toward home. He would move on a gradual angle that would eventually take him out of the dune and back onto the beach well before he reached Cape Henry and the settlement.

The dune grass was thick here and taller than Jonathan, but he was confident he was walking in the correct direction. At times, he used his walking stick to part the grass ahead of him. He heard the sea birds above and looked up in time to see five pelicans in their V formation begin to drop down from their altitude of about 100 feet. He wished he could see the Bay at that point because he loved how pelicans leveled off and maintained their formation only inches above the surface of the water.

I'll see it the next time I'm on the beach, he thought.

But there would be no next time. Jonathan wouldn't get back to the beach today. He wouldn't make it through the dune grass. Today would be different.

He stopped walking somewhere midway in the dune when he noticed a dead raccoon, about three feet ahead of him. He poked at the carcass with his walking stick. It was more of a pelt than a carcass. Jonathan could tell there was no skeleton under the skin. The head and skull appeared intact. Another poke with his stick and the animal's head rolled slightly toward him revealing two blood-red eyes. The animal's skeleton and, it would seem, all internal organs were gone in a remarkably bloodless scene.

Jonathan didn't know what to make of it. He was tempted to bring the carcass home for his father to examine, but he knew at least two reasons for not touching a dead animal found on the ground. Another animal—possibly the one responsible for the found animal's death—might be lurking nearby ready to reclaim its kill. From the looks of the raccoon, Jonathan doubted that was the case. Even the scavenger birds had no interest. He also heard talk among the adults in the settlement that Tommy Albright's father got the fever when he picked up an animal he found dead in the woods. It nearly killed him.

Jonathan turned from the raccoon because something else drew him deeper into the dune. He moved slowly, but stopped again when he noticed an opening in the sand. It wasn't very large, but easily big enough for it to have been the entrance to the raccoon's home.

Do raccoons live in the sand? he wondered.

It was an unseasonably warm day in early June, but

Jonathan could feel that the air coming from the opening was warmer than the outside air. It was damp, as well. The opening was upwind of Jonathan. The slight breeze brought the heat and a stale smell to him. He felt it getting warmer, now hot, and the smell was unmistakable. It was the odor of animal decomposition. No mistaking it.

"Smell it once and you'll never forget," his dad had taught him.

And then he heard it. It was a kind of rumbling sound. It was clearly coming from inside the opening. Jonathan tried, but he couldn't see any shape within the hole. The darkness was darker than anything he could remember. It was like looking into nothing. And then he saw them. Two red dots. They were somewhere close to the center of the blackness of the opening. Other than the dead raccoon, Jonathan had never seen an animal with red eyes. But, if they really were eyes, he knew an attack could be imminent.

Jonathan's sense of adventure shifted to a feeling of fear. Despite a sudden rubbery sensation in his legs, he took another step forward. And then, another. At some point, he took the irreversible step. Turning away and fleeing directly to the beach was now no longer an option. He didn't know when that moment occurred. He would never know.

The rumbling sound became the howl of a very strong wind. Jonathan held out his hands in an effort to shield his face from the increased flow of much hotter air emitted by the opening. He felt his arms being pulled toward it.

How can I be pulled toward the opening, when it's blowing hot air in my face with so much force? The confused thought crossed his mind.

He tried to scream, but he was only able to gasp for air. Despite his resistance, his body began to lean toward the opening. His shoes, suspended by their laces from his shoulder, flew off and landed well beyond the opening. Jonathan's walking stick, wrenched from his hand, flew six feet beyond the opening. It imbedded itself more than half its length into the sand.

Jonathan now leaned radically toward the opening. He appeared oddly taller—or maybe the right word is *longer*. From his ankles to his hair, which extended straight out from the top of his head, his stretched body was now almost parallel to the surface of the dune. Were he not in such obvious pain, his appearance would have been comical. Cartoonish. It was as though he no longer had a skeletal structure to maintain the integrity of his body. He was being drawn closer and closer to the opening. Eventually, his feet were pulled off the ground.

Then, there was quiet.

Jonathan's body lay on the ground at the apron of the opening in the dune. Much like the raccoon he had spotted earlier, his head appeared uninjured, except for his very bloodshot eyes, open in a vacuous stare. His otherwise relaxed facial expression belied his struggle with the opening that occurred moments before his death. His pants and shirt looked less like they covered a human body and more like they were lying flat on the sand. Like the raccoon again, all bones, organs, and bodily fluids appeared to have been sucked out of him.

His skin remained with no stain of blood, but Jonathan was gone.

The world is a dangerous place,
not because of those who do evil,
but because of those who look and do nothing.

Albert Einstein

A Monday in Early June
2010

1

"You do know you're breaking the law, right?"

The teenage girl in the dune looked up in the direction of the three-story building. She was pretty sure the voice came from either the second or third floor.

The breeze out of the north was at her back, making it hard for her to hear clearly. She fought the late morning sunlight shining in her face as she looked up. She had stopped walking a few feet shy of the shadow cast by the condo building that housed the voice.

"What did you say? I can't really see you because of the glare," she said.

"I asked if you knew you were breaking the law." This time a little louder.

Shielding her eyes and squinting to see the speaker more clearly, she said, "What are you talking about? Am I doing something wrong? It's not illegal to walk on the beach, is it?"

"It's the dune, young lady. I'm talking about the dune. It's against the law to traipse through the dune like that."

"Huh? You're kidding, right?"

"Nope. Serious as a heart attack," he said.

"What's so special about the dune?"

"Dune's the only thing keeping the Bay from swallowing this building and all the other Bayfront places. When a storm kicks up, the Bay gets angry. I can't tell you how many times I've seen the water come up to the edge of the dune. Been here through a few tropical storms and even a minor hurricane. The water's come up to where you are standing—maybe a little further."

The young woman looked down and took a few steps forward, into the shadow of the building. The glare was no longer a factor. She looked over her shoulder to the southern edge of the Chesapeake Bay and the expanse of dune through which she had already walked.

"We ever get a direct hit from a big hurricane," the old man continued, now much more easily heard, "I hate to think what it would mean. Probably destroy the whole dune and kick the snot out of this property. 'Course, if enough people screw up the area by taking nature walks, we won't have to wait for a direct hit from a storm."

"Yeah, I get it. But I really don't think I *screwed up* the area by walking here."

"You never know. I'm sure you don't mean any harm, but still…"

"So, what should I do now…stand here and become part of the dune?" she held her arms out from her sides, a pair of flip-flops hanging from the fingers of her right hand.

The old man smiled. His teeth seemed to shine. They contrasted with his mostly gray beard and his similarly colored thick head of hair which appeared to have successfully resisted any effort to brush it.

Every generation of teenagers believes it discovered sarcasm, he thought. *Let's see how she handles a taste of her own medicine.*

"Sure. That would be great. Pretty girl like you would spruce up the appearance of the dune. Tell you what—I'll toss you a sandwich for lunch and another at dinner time."

"What about breakfast tomorrow? What are you serving then?" the sarcasm continued.

"You really don't know much about the dune, do you? If you tried to spend the night where you're standing, my young friend, it's possible you wouldn't be there in the morning."

She decided to implement a temporary ceasefire in the sarcasm battle. She didn't know what to make of his last comment.

"So, I'll tell you what. I'm going to go out the way I came in. Is that all right with you?"

"No. Wait. That doesn't make any sense. You're just about through it now. Best to keep walking forward and step up on our little boardwalk, right there in front of you. You can use the crosswalk over there (he pointed to his left) to get over the dune and back on the beach."

The young woman walked slowly through the remaining dune, lifting her feet high, accentuating her steps artificially to send the message that she was not harming any plant life.

The old man noted her silent sarcasm and decided to keep the game going.

"Are you sure you're being careful enough? Watch where you step." He wondered if she noticed he had nearly laughed aloud when he spoke this time.

"I am. *I* am." She knew he couldn't see her rolling her eyes in reaction to his comments.

"Say, what's your name, anyway?" he asked.

"Malia. Malia Matthews."

"Malia. Sounds Hawaiian."

"That's what it is."

"You don't look Hawaiian."

"I'm not. I was born in Hawaii. My dad was in the Army."

"Assigned to Schofield Barracks?"

"Right again," she said.

"Well, Malia Matthews, shouldn't you be in school today? Summer break hasn't started yet, has it?"

"No. I'm a senior at Cox High School. This is exam week."

"Okay, then. Why aren't you in school taking an exam?"

"I had an exam this morning."

"And what about tomorrow? Shouldn't you be studying? Is it Test-free Tuesday or something?"

"That's pretty funny. I have another exam tomorrow morning, but I'm exempt from the afternoon exam," she said.

"Exempt. Really? You must be pretty smart."

"I suppose. And I bet I know what you're going to say next."

"Oh, really? What am I going to say?"

"You're going to say, 'Pretty smart, but not smart enough to know not to walk in the dune.' Am I right?"

"Good for you, Malia Matthews. You're smart *and* funny. Actually, I hadn't thought of that. That would be a bit too sarcastic even for me. Or, as you might say, a bit too snarky."

A brief moment passed with neither of them speaking.

"Here's another question for you. Let me test your Hawaiian knowledge," Bob spoke again.

"I haven't been there since I was two years old, but I'll try."

"Do you know what a lanai is?"

"Of course. You're standing on one," she replied.

"Good for you. I can't get my neighbors to use the term, but you nailed it. You see, I spent some time in Hawaii myself when I was in the Navy."

"My turn to guess: Pearl Harbor?"

"You got it," he said.

"Hey, is that a dog looking at me?"

The old man's dog had put its head between the bars of the balcony's railing.

"It's so cute. I love the way its tongue is sticking out like that," she said.

"Don't give him too many compliments. It'll go to his head."

"What kind of dog is it? It looks like a Yorkie."

"No. This little mop is Pepper. He's a Havenese."

"A what?"

"Havenese. It's the national dog of Cuba. I've had him for nearly seven years. He's good company for an old fart like me and he's pretty easy to take care of."

"Are they smart dogs?"

"He has his stupid moments, but, yeah, I guess he's pretty smart. Of course, he's never been exempted from any high school exams."

They exchanged smiles.

"Smart enough to stay out of the dune?" she asked.

The old man returned Malia's smile and said, "As a matter of fact, he is. I can't remember a time he wandered into the dune."

"Okay, let me ask you a question," she said.

"Shoot."

"Well, I know Pepper's name, but I don't know yours."

"That really isn't a question, you know, but I'll gladly tell you my name. It's Bob. Bob Meissner. Around here most people call me The Commodore."

"The *what* door? What kind of a nickname is that?"

"Ha! That's me. I'm the door to the commode. No, Malia, it's Commodore. It's an old Navy designation. Not exactly a rank, but something like that. You see, I'm an old salt. Many years, and many pounds ago, I was a sailor. I'll tell you what, you can call me Commodore, if you want, but I'm fine if you just call me Bob."

"Commodore Bob. I like that. So, you're the salt and the dog is the pepper."

"Good for you. Most people never figure out how he got his name."

"Commodore Bob, can I ask you a question?"

"Another question? Sure."

"Did you mean it when you said that about the dune?"

"When I said what about the dune? About how important it is? Darn right I was serious. That dune has saved this property more than once and it'll do it again unless people keep…"

"No, Commodore," she cut him off. "Not that. I get that part. What did you mean when you said I wouldn't be here in the morning if I tried to spend the night in the dune?"

"Well, you might, I suppose. I guess nothing is one hundred percent, but dunes are special places. There are a lot of stories connected to this dune. Dunes can be dangerous. I don't think it would be safe for you overnight—especially this week."

"Why, because I'm a helpless little girl?" She exaggerated her voice to make her point.

"Malia Matthews, I've known you for all of about five minutes, but I already know you are anything but a helpless little girl."

"Okay, so what's the mystery? And what's so special

about this week?"

"What's so special about this week? I can't give you a good answer. I can only tell you that I'm getting a sense that the dune is angry or particularly unwelcoming this week. Does that sound crazy?"

"A little, I guess. Hey, are you trying to scare me to see if I'm brave enough to spend a night in the dune," she said.

"Oh, God, no. From what I've been able to learn, the dune isn't very kind to people who invade its space. It can be unforgiving but, thanks to Mother Nature, it is very resilient. I think its expectation is that we show our gratitude for the protection it provides by leaving it alone."

"You make it sound alive, Commodore." She was now standing on the narrow walkway composed of wooden deck planks that stretched the length of the property bordering the dune, separating it from Bob's building. She could see him clearly now, as he leaned over the third-floor balcony railing. His hair moved with the breeze and his weathered face was rich with lines of age and experience.

She supposed he was well into his eighties, but she also knew young people were notoriously bad at guessing the ages of most adults—especially the elderly. Her grandfather died two years ago, when he was seventy-nine. To her, Bob looked older than her grandfather.

"Now, Malia Matthews, there is no way a smart girl like you could have walked through that wonderful stretch of dune without feeling how alive it is."

"Well, there are things growing in there, but I don't think that's what you mean. Do you think the dune is living? Like it has a personality?"

"Do you have a problem with that?"

"I guess not. It's just that…"

"Tell you what," he interrupted her. "If you have time

between studying for exams, do some research. Learn more about dunes. We'll talk the next time you come around."

"Deal. Like I said, I have an exam tomorrow morning. I won't be able to be here until after lunch. I don't know exactly what time, especially if I get stuck in the library doing all this research." Malia smiled. She was clearly enjoying her conversation with the old man, but she still wasn't sure if he was totally serious or maybe even a little loopy.

"No matter. I'll be here."

"Okay, Commodore Bob. I'll see you and Pepper tomorrow."

"Sure. If not tomorrow, then another day. We'll be here."

"I think I'll walk down to the crosswalk to get back on the beach."

"Thank you, Malia."

She dropped her flip-flops onto the wood planks of the walkway, stepped into them, and began slowly walking away."

"Say, Malia," he said.

"Yes, sir?" She stopped, turned, and looked up at him.

"When you do your dune research, don't forget to see what Marco Polo has to say about the dunes."

"Really? Okay." She started walking again.

"You *do* know who…"

"Who Marco Polo is? Yes, Commodore, I know who Marco Polo is." She waved goodbye without turning to face him. "I'm pretty smart. Remember? You said so yourself."

"That's good. Hey, Malia?" he said.

"Yes, sir?" she slowed her pace, but kept walking. There was a touch of exasperation in her voice.

"Marco," he said.

Her laugh was almost a giggle. She hunched her shoulders slightly, but still did not turn to look at him. Her exasperation vanished.

"Polo," she replied.

"Marco."

"Polo."

"Marco," he said again.

"I'll see you tomorrow, Commodore Bob."

"I hope so," he said aloud, but to himself. Malia was nearly at the crosswalk and out of earshot.

2

The exchange with Malia was the highlight of Bob's day. But, at the same time, their encounter troubled him. He was pretty good when it came to reading people, but he didn't know what to make of her. Talking to her made him somehow uneasy. He'd had this feeling before—more times than he cared to remember. He couldn't put his finger on it, but this time the feeling was stronger, stranger, and unsettling.

Something's wrong here. Something's really screwed up, he thought.

It didn't make a lot of sense that his conversation with a bright, young high schooler left him so much on guard. The timing of it raised a few red flags. Days ago, he began to sense something dangerous in the dune. And now, in the very same dune, he sees Malia. He couldn't shake the feeling that nothing good would come from all this.

Nothing good is one thing, but this feels different...worse, maybe even evil, he said to himself.

He reached for his hooded sweatshirt and zipped it halfway up. The thought gave him a chill.

I'm probably jumping to conclusions.

Probably, but Bob was concerned enough to consider not being available the next time Malia came to the beach. In fact, he really wasn't sure she would return, despite what she had said. Why would she come back? He said he would be here whenever she returned. She probably figured that was just Bob's way of making conversation.

Bob also wondered if he might have come across as

being a little creepy.

An old man warning a young girl about the dangers of the dune? That even seems creepy to me, he thought.

Still he worried where all this would lead. For now, he would keep his concerns to himself.

"That's a laugh," he said aloud to no one. "Who on earth would I share them with, anyway?"

"How about you, Pepper?" he said to the dog. "Can you keep a secret?"

He tried to reassure himself. *Malia's just a kid, a good kid. Or am I jumping to conclusions about her as well?*

He didn't think he was, but he knew himself well. In his long life, he was always willing to give people another chance and it often blew up in his face. He carried the scars of past encounters. Past betrayals.

As he progressed through the ranks, he had given sailors second chances and forgiven minor infractions. Often, he was gratified to see a young service member demonstrate the potential to be a good sailor. Naturally, there were occasions when a sailor disappointed Bob by taking advantage of his willingness to clear the slate, only to violate the rules or break the law again. He never considered it too big a price to pay. It was just his nature.

We're all alike. Look past the flaws and see the good in a person. I'd want to be given a break and the benefit of the doubt.

If he was wrong about Malia, it wouldn't be the first time. Was she a source of trouble or was she in some way at great risk? Maybe, but maybe she was simply a young girl walking in the dune.

You're getting way ahead of yourself again, old man. You just met the kid.

The day's western sky presented Bob with a sunset he

could admire. As the sun met the horizon behind the span of the Chesapeake Bay Bridge-Tunnel closest to Virginia Beach, the sky was a vibrant red and orange on a blue backdrop. The evening air felt suddenly free of all humidity. Bob was grateful for the change in the weather. It was welcome news for an old salt who felt an inexplicable need to spend a good part of the night on watch here on the balcony.

He wasn't sure if he was protecting the dune from harm or if he was supposed to be on guard for a specific danger coming from the dune. He feared the latter. The dune was trying to tell him something. He was sure of it. When he met Malia, she was in the dune.

Is there a message in that? he wondered. *Is Malia the messenger? Is Malia the message? Is this all bullshit?*

"Don't ask me what I'm looking for," he said aloud to the looming night sky, as he leaned on the balcony railing and looked into the dune. "I guess it's like the Supreme Court said about porn: I'll know it when I see it. At least, I think I will."

*The only thing necessary for the triumph of evil
is for good men to do nothing.*

Edmund Burke

Tuesday

3

The sound of the approaching dump truck caused Pepper to stir in his master's lap. The dog's movement, more so than its soft growl, was enough to wake Bob. Each morning, the city truck rode along the beach, tying off and removing trash bags from the containers placed every hundred yards or so apart along the edge where the beach meets the dune. The two-person crew would then line each steel can with a new plastic bag and toss in a healthy handful of sand to prevent the bag from billowing out due to a strong gust. There was a rhythm to the repetitive nature of their work. They went from trashcan to trashcan quickly and efficiently.

Bob was initially disoriented when he awoke. His confusion quickly gave way to annoyance when he realized he was in a chair on his balcony. He hadn't planned to spend the entire night waiting for something to happen in the dune, but here he was. His vigil had been interrupted, at some point, by sleep.

And it wasn't a very good sleep. Bob was achy and cranky. Years ago, standing an all-night watch at sea was less of a challenge.

"Well, that wasn't one of my brighter ideas," he said. Standing now, Bob stared out over the balcony railing. His sense that there was something ominous in the dune had not lessened. He scanned the dune for any sign of change from the day before, but saw none.

I guess if anything dramatic had happened last night, Pepper would have alerted me, he thought. He looked down at the curled up dog who had apparently gone back to sleep.

"Who am I kidding?" Bob said aloud. "You'd probably

sleep through an earthquake if it happened when you considered yourself off duty."

Sensing the words were directed to him, Pepper lifted his head and looked at Bob.

"You wouldn't let me down. Would you, old dog?" he said to Pepper. "Of course, you *did* let me fall asleep out here last night."

Not surprisingly, the dog looked up, now fully aware that Bob was talking to him. The tone of his voice was enough to make Pepper wag his tail casually and stay with Bob as he walked the length of the balcony to stretch his legs after a night in the chair.

"Man, am I stiff this morning," he said.

At one end of the balcony was a door to an exposed back stairwell. It was one of three similar arrangements to accommodate easy beach access for the eighteen units in the building. The stairs led to the boardwalk on which Malia had stood the day before. When Bob opened the door, Pepper ran down the stairs, lifted his leg on a decorative plant at the corner of the building, and returned promptly to the third floor balcony. This was their morning routine, but it was probably the only condo rule Bob ignored with impunity.

```
Bay Ridge Condominiums Rule #43,
paragraph 3B: All dogs must be on a
leash when not in their condo units.
No dog is permitted to relieve itself
on the boardwalk area.
```

Bob secured the stairwell door once Pepper had returned. He then opened the sliding glass door and walked into his condo.

Just as his cup of coffee finished brewing and the toast popped up—slightly burned—the way he liked it, a thought occurred to him. It wiped away any remaining sleepiness.

What if Malia had returned to the dune last night, after I fell asleep? he thought. *The news says high school kids sneak out on their parents all the time. She said my warnings made her curious.*

"Damn!" Bob picked up the coffee cup and moved quickly to the balcony. He leaned over the railing and stared with more intensity than before, determined to identify any changes in its appearance from the previous day. At this point, he figured he knew that patch of dune better than anyone on earth.

If there was something out of the ordinary in the dune that morning, Bob didn't see it. A part of him was reassured, concluding nothing bad occurred last night. His less forgiving side reminded him that sleeping all night on the balcony was a dumb thing for a man his age to do.

Bob knew, if he was lucky, he was making a lot more than was warranted about his premonition regarding the dune. Throughout his life, however, he had learned time and again to trust his gut. As a young ensign he learned reliance on luck was foolish. Hoping for the best was fine, but preparing for the worst was always the best advice he gave himself and others.

Still, a morning mostly spent scouring the dune from his third floor balcony—sometimes using binoculars—uncovered no evidence of unusual overnight activity. There was a second cup of coffee. And a third. Bob puttered around, doing minor chores. He moved a load of laundry from the hamper to the washing machine and restocked the refrigerator with iced teas and Diet Pepsis. He didn't allow himself to linger too long before returning to the balcony, usually with a snack of some kind in his hand.

When he wasn't peering into the dune, Bob enjoyed the dolphins passing in the Bay. Their smooth movement as they cut through the water gave him a sense of calm, much needed after his disappointment from the night before. There seemed to be more dolphins than usual this morning.

A sense of duty forced him to shift his gaze frequently back to the dune. He didn't know what he hoped to see, but he did not want to risk missing anything significant.

His concentration was broken when Pepper whimpered loud enough to get his attention. The dog sat at the balcony door, clearly signaling it wanted to go downstairs again. Bob looked at his watch and was surprised to learn it was nearly 1:30 in the afternoon. Bob had never been much of a lunch eater. His preference was to graze throughout the late morning and early afternoon eating fruit, peanuts, and an occasional chocolate chip cookie. As a result, mid-afternoons often snuck up on him.

"Not this time, buddy," Bob said as he slid open the glass door. Pepper followed him inside. "Nah, this time we go out front on the leash. I owe you your morning walk, even if it isn't morning any more. But it has to be a quick one because I've got to get back on watch on the lanai. You should want to get back, too. Your girlfriend might be coming back to see you."

Pepper cooperated by quickly taking care of business as soon as they crossed the parking lot and reached the street. Bob deposited the poop bag in one of the receptacles provided by the community. In less than fifteen minutes, they were back in the condo. Bob gave Pepper a treat and returned to the balcony. He left the door open just enough for the dog to join him.

Bob recalled Malia indicated she would not be able to return until after lunch, but he really wondered if she would be coming at all.

Maybe she changed her mind about revisiting, he thought. *Wouldn't blame her if she did.*

"There's no way she enjoyed our conversation as much as I did," he said in a low voice to Pepper. "Old fart like me."

This round of introspection caused him to wonder

again if something might have happened to her in the dune overnight. As he continued to look into the dune, he tried to put the thought out of his mind by telling himself she was home last night, studying for her exam. She was too smart to do something so risky, especially during exam week. Besides, she really did seem to be a responsible kid. Still, he might have unintentionally made the dunes appear to be more of an adventure than a danger.

Bob knew he would have to see Malia walking on the beach to be sure she was okay.

4

The dune was without shadows thanks to the afternoon sun. Bob was standing, resting his forearms on the balcony railing when he saw Malia walking slowly along the beach. He felt an immediate sense of relief. She was a good distance off to the east.

He made no sign to get her attention, but simply watched her. She appeared lost in thought as she reached a point directly in front of him. He wasn't about to yell to her. If she had something on her mind or if she was actually walking to a destination other than his boardwalk, he wasn't going to interfere.

Malia continued walking along the beach, only a step or two away from the small waves breaking on the southern shore of the Chesapeake Bay. Due north, across the Bay some two hundred miles, was the city of Baltimore and the mouth of the Susquehanna River, one of more than 150 rivers that fed the Bay. Malia hardly seemed to notice the waves.

Bob watched Malia walk past him and then stop. She was looking down at the sand. Through the binoculars, he could see her head bobbing slightly. He couldn't help but think she was talking to herself. The sight of a pod of dolphins gliding from west to east, about as close to the shore as he had ever seen, completely distracted him.

Bob's mind went back to his active Navy days when his ship would encounter dolphins at sea and when they seemed to dance around the ship as it slowed to sail safely into a port.

He recalled his combat-related deployments and the

calm gracefulness of the dolphins despite the tenseness of the tactical situation. As a young officer, he assumed the dolphins were unaware of the danger in the waters they shared with the US Navy. Over the years, he had developed a better appreciation for the contrast presented between peaceful and destructive use of the oceans. But those were now the musings of an old man who was lost in his thoughts.

As the last of the pod swam into the distance, Bob shifted his attention back to the beach where he had seen Malia stop. She was no longer there. He looked well down the beach. No sign of her.

Either she picked up her pace, he thought, *or....*

"Marco."

He looked down to the narrow boardwalk between his condo and the dune. He smiled.

"Polo."

"Hello, Commodore Bob," Malia said.

"I thought I told you it was okay to call me Bob," he said.

"I know. I looked up info on dunes like you said, but I decided to find out more about commodores," she responded.

"And what did you learn?"

"Well, I learned that you either had a long career in the Navy or you were a part of a group that played backup music for somebody named Lionel Richie."

"Oh, Malia Matthews, you make this old man laugh. You have a good sense of humor. That's important. Don't let anyone take it away from you."

"My grandpa used to tell me the same thing."

"A wise man, your grandpa. Say, I saw you walking

along the beach. I thought you were going to just keep on going. Everything okay?"

"What? Oh, yeah. I was going over my Biology final in my head and I think I got a question wrong."

"Only one?"

"Only one that I can remember."

"Smart girl, you are."

"Now you sound like Yoda. Yoda is the…"

"Whoa there, young lady. Just like you and Marco Polo, I know all about Yoda. Speaking of Mr. Polo, what did you learn about him and the dunes?"

"You know, Commodore Bob, there are a couple of picnic tables and benches right there at the end of the crossover." She pointed to her right. "We could sit there and talk, if you want."

"Maybe next time, Malia. Today I'm dedicating as much time as I can to keeping an eye on the dune. I don't want to wander away if I can help it. I think there's something in there I need to see."

"Well, that sounds mysterious. Is there something in there I should know about?" She made air quotes with her hands when she echoed Bob's words, *something in there.*

"Let's just say I'm pretty sure there's something in there you shouldn't know about. I stayed out here a good part of the night thinking I might see something."

"And?"

"Nothing worth talking about."

"Not fair, Commodore Bob. You do know you're making me more curious about the dune when you talk that way."

"Well, if you must know the truth, I fell asleep."

"Oh, no! Don't tell me you spent the night on your balcony…excuse me…your lanai."

"Yes I did and I'm embarrassed to have to admit it. So, we can talk about all that another time, Malia. For now, tell me about Marco Polo."

"Hello, Pepper!" Malia said when Pepper's head appeared through the railings.

"And rather than wake me up so we could both sleep inside in a comfortable bed, this knucklehead curled up in my lap and never woke up until early this morning."

"At least you had your protector with you," she said.

"Oh, yeah, some protection he would be."

"So, Commodore, did you know Marco Polo personally? The stuff I read about him and the dunes sounds a lot like the things you said yesterday."

"Oh, sure. We double-dated to our high school prom. Do you realize how long ago Marco Polo lived?"

"I know. I was just kidding."

"Well, what did you learn?"

"Marco Polo believed dunes were alive with spirits," she began.

"That's right. That's what he wrote," Bob said.

"But he was talking about the dunes in a desert and the sounds they made. He wasn't talking about a sand dune near the Chesapeake Bay in Virginia Beach."

"Where did you read that? He was relating what he saw and heard in his travels. I don't think he ruled out the dune at any beach, let alone Virginia Beach."

"Are you sure you didn't know him? Maybe you two had a play date when you were kids?"

Her smile was infectious and Bob couldn't help but

notice how brightly the sunlight reflected in her eyes.

"Malia, did you read *about* him or did you read Marco Polo's own words?"

"Both. I read a couple of things about him, but I also read part of his journal."

"*The Travels of Marco Polo.*"

"Yes," Malia said.

"Good. Then you know that he didn't just call them spirits. He called them evil spirits."

"Yeah, well. I also read that scientists have explained how the sounds are made. It's all about shifting sands, the wind, and even the size of the grains of sand rubbing against each other. If Marco Polo knew that, I doubt he would have believed the sounds were made by evil spirits."

"It isn't only the sounds that caused him to think the way he did. But, I can see you're a skeptic. And at such a young age! You think this is all nonsense. Don't you?"

"Commodore, I'm not a baby. I don't keep a light on at night and it's been a long time since my dad had to check under the bed before I would go to sleep."

"Hmm. Are you saying you don't believe in spirits or you don't believe in evil?"

"I don't know. I guess…"

"It isn't only Marco Polo and stories about faraway places. There are people who are convinced all dunes, to include this one right here, hold some kind of evil or are cursed in some way."

"Seriously? How?"

"Well, did you know that forty years ago, or so, on this property where the high-class Bay Ridge Condominium complex sits (Bob puffed out his chest, to emphasize his intentional, false bravado), there was a sleazy, run-down motel?"

"Okay," she slowly said.

"Yeah, not the kind of place a family would want to stay. Late one night, the desk clerk was murdered. Nothing was stolen. He was just found dead. Some people swear his ghost is still on the property."

"I could understand that, if I believed in ghosts," she said.

"And you don't?"

"I don't know. I've never seen one, but I can't prove there aren't any."

"Malia, almost every summer there are stories in the news—at least one or two—about a kid who goes missing here in Virginia Beach. Sometimes, the report indicates the person was last seen in a dune. Other times, they don't really say. The most mysterious cases seem to deal with kids your age or a little older. Can't predict when. Doesn't seem to have anything to do with bad weather or a full moon or anything like that. All I know is these things happen again and again."

"And you blame the dune?"

"I don't know who or what to blame. I just don't like it when there is no reasonable explanation when something awful happens—especially to a kid. Most of the time, the police conclude the kid had been drinking, wandered off, and drowned in the Bay."

"Don't you think that could happen?"

"Oh, sure. But not every time. No way."

"Commodore, I really need to head home soon," Malia said after checking the time on her phone. "How about one more story? Maybe an old sailor's tale about the ocean or the Bay."

"Malia, there's a lifetime of stories about strange things that have happened at sea and in these very waters. Let's see. Only one more story, right?" He was quiet for a few seconds, searching his memory. "Oh, how could I forget?" He paused again. "You know, maybe I'd better not. The story I had in mind is a little too…"

"Too scary for a little girl? Come on, Commodore. Now you have to tell me," she countered.

"Have you ever heard about the Ash Wednesday storm of 1962?"

"No, but I don't want to hear about a storm. I want you to tell me the other story. The one you were about to tell me," Malia said.

"This *is* the *other* story, Malia," he replied.

"Oh, sorry. No, I've never heard of that storm."

"It was a classic nor'easter. And you know how bad they can be around here. Well, this storm rode right up the coast. It hit Virginia Beach on March 6th, Ash Wednesday that year, and stuck around for three days. The waves were thirty feet high and they battered the coast through five high tides!"

"That must have been scary." Malia understood Bob's enthusiasm for the longevity and severity of the storm. His narrative didn't frighten her, but she made the conscious decision to call it scary because she thought Bob had arrived at the point of his story. She had no idea what was to come.

"It did tremendous damage to a lot of houses and the landscape. It was terrible. There are photos of it on the Internet. You ought to check them out."

"I will. I promise. Well, thank you, Commodore Bob for the stories. I ought to be…"

"Don't you want to hear the whole story?"

"There's more?"

"Let me get to the point because I know you have to go home. Well, as the storm continued, for some reason, people were drawn to the dune. This dune, right here. Whatever they found in there either drove them crazy or scared them so badly they walked out of the dune, across the beach, and into the Chesapeake Bay. When the storm finally passed, more than two dozen bodies washed ashore at Norfolk Naval Base. Their eyeballs were bright red and it looked as though their insides had been sucked right out of their bodies. When sailors tried to recover their remains from the beach, the bodies essentially disintegrated into dust or sand."

"Are you serious? I've never heard that story. Is it true?"

"As you get older, Malia, you'll discover that not everything that is true can be proven with the tools we have available. The storm cannot be denied. The locals continue to talk about the incident, but the government denies it ever happened. So, I guess, the lesson to my story is that you shouldn't let yourself be fooled, dear girl. There is evil in the world and there's danger in the dune."

"Are you sure you aren't just trying to scare me, Commodore Bob. Because you have."

"I just want to be sure you and your friends have a healthy respect for the dune."

"Oh, I think I got that message, Commodore," she said.

Bob wasn't sure if Malia truly understood his message. In addition to respecting the dune's protective role, there was good reason to fear its potential for no good. She may not be convinced, but he knew there was something there. He was content to call it a spirit. If the term was good enough for Marco Polo, it was good enough for Bob. More importantly, he was convinced whatever it is, it should also be called evil.

Malia told him she had two exams the next day and one each on Thursday and Friday.

"I'm not sure when I will be able to come back," she said.

"No worries, Malia. Pepper and I will be here if you do."

"Oh, I'll definitely be back. Would it be okay if I brought a friend with me next time?"

"Do you think any of your friends could stand an old man who will yell at them if they don't stay out of the dune?"

"Absolutely. But I have one condition," she said.

"What's that?"

"You and Pepper have to come down to the picnic table over there." She pointed to the part of the walkway that intersected with the crossover to the beach. "Commodore? Commodore Bob? Did you hear what I just said?"

"What? Oh, yeah. I'm sorry. Something got my attention. Yes. I agree. Next time I'll drag my tired old bones all the way down there," he said.

"My grandma always says, *the walk will do me good,*" Malia said.

"She's right," he said, but he was clearly distracted by something he saw (or thought he saw) in the dune. "Grandmas are always right."

"Okay, Commodore Bob. I have to get going."

"Be careful, Malia. See you soon." His attention remained on the dune.

Malia walked the length of the boardwalk, used the crossover, and began walking east on the beach. Several times during her departure, she looked into the dune and back at Bob. The expression on her face was one of concerned confusion.

When she crossed in front of his condo unit, she waved from the beach. Pepper barked once in her direction, but the Bob's focus was on the dune.

He wasn't sure what he had seen, but something—some

movement—in the dune grabbed his attention. He was determined to identify it.

He wondered if Malia noticed his sudden disconnect from the conversation. He was pretty sure she had. His behavior must have caught her off guard. He could tell she was unsure how to handle his unexpected distraction. He was relieved she didn't press him for an explanation. He wasn't sure how he would describe the instant chill that came over him, why he disengaged so abruptly from their conversation, or why he was unable to take his eyes off the dune.

She probably picked up on all of that, he thought.

5

Bob eventually looked up from the dune. Malia was long gone when he did. He scanned the beach, but there was no sign of her. A middle-aged woman was tossing a tennis ball that her black lab willingly retrieved. Bob was amused at how eagerly the dog chased the flight of the ball—whether along the beach or into the Bay.

"No way you'd get those dainty paws wet in the Bay, old dog," he said. Pepper had curled up under the table on the balcony. The dog's only reaction to the comment was to shift his eyes in Bob's direction before reclosing them.

A man and a woman, probably in their sixties, walked slowly hand-in-hand in the sand. Bob thought they looked familiar, but he couldn't be sure.

Even in early June, the weekday crowd at the beach was light. Once school was out for the summer, the daily population would grow, but it would never approach the size of the crowds at the oceanfront. Most Virginia Beach residents were unaware there was a public beach here. It got busier on weekends, but it was almost exclusively a neighborhood crowd. There wasn't a lot of on-the-street parking. Most people who used the beach either lived Bayfront or within easy walking distance.

"Hellooo, Commodore," the woman on the beach yelled, waving a hand well above her head. Her hand waving caught his attention. He heard her extended shout of the word, 'hello' and knew the next word started with a 'K' or a 'hard C.'

Pepper stood and moved to the railing as Bob squinted to identify the woman.

"Why, hello, Mary," he said, doubting his voice was strong enough to carry as far as hers. "I didn't know you were back in town. I can't believe you got the old paisano out for a walk." It always made Bob happy when the Castalanos returned to Virginia Beach.

Tony and Mary Castalano were two of the many part-time residents in Bob's building. They owned a second floor end unit and typically spent winters in Florida, returning to Virginia Beach each year, soon after Memorial Day. Tony made sure they spent at least 183 days in Florida every calendar year to ensure he could claim Florida residency and avoid Virginia state taxes.

Bob met Tony and Mary a decade ago at the condo's community pool. He interrupted the couple's conversation when he overheard Tony's accent.

"Excuse me. Are you from New Jersey?"

"Yeah. How did you know?" Tony said.

"Your accent, my friend. It isn't the strongest I've ever heard, but it's classic."

"What accent?" Tony asked, tongue-in-cheek.

"Right. Of course. What accent? I was thinking Jersey or New York."

"Nah. If I was from New York, I would have told you to go screw yourself right from the start," Tony said.

"What if I guessed Philly?"

"Your ass would be in the pool by now."

"I'm Bob Meissner," he said, offering his right hand. "I served with a lot of guys from New Jersey, New York, and even Philly during my years in the Navy. They were almost all good guys and great sailors. But, most of all, I just always loved the way they talked."

"Yeah, even though I don't hear it in my voice anymore, I guess I'll never lose all of my Jersey accent."

Tony told Bob that he and Mary met at Saint Peter's College in Jersey City. After graduation, Tony had a successful IT career in the private sector and taught Computer Science as an adjunct professor at a New Jersey community college.

For her part, Mary majored in Elementary Education and had a full career in various teaching positions at the kindergarten, first, and second grade levels.

Several vacations in Virginia Beach resulted in their buying a place in the Bay Ridge Condominiums, which they kept when they decided to leave New Jersey and make Florida their home of record.

"Don't take this the wrong way, Tony, but you don't strike me as the academic type," Bob said.

"I'll take that to mean I've never lost the common touch," Tony said. "I'm a city kid who grew up in a tough neighborhood. College was my way out. I say my childhood taught me to look people directly in the eye and not down my nose."

"We're going to get along just fine," Bob replied. "Say, Tony, I know we just met, but I've got to tell you that's one hell of a scar you've got on your chest. Makes the line from my bypass surgery look flimsy."

That's when Bob learned Tony was a heart transplant recipient.

"Yeah, I'm not really crazy about it, but the docs told me it was a new heart or a casket," Tony said.

"Ha! Sounds like you made the right choice."

Tony and Bob spent the rest of the day trading stories and telling jokes. They talked about sports, politics, and the sad state of the world.

"You're a straight shooter, Tony. I like that in a man," Bob told him as their initial encounter at the pool came to a close. They had been friends ever since. Somewhere along the way, Bob began referring to Tony as his "paisano."

Bob was right. His voice did not project well enough for Mary to hear more than a few words. Nonetheless, she smiled broadly, nodded, and waved again.

"Come by later for a drink," she said before turning with her husband to continue their walk.

Bob's attention was brought back to the dune by Pepper. Almost immediately after the Castalanos resumed their walk, Pepper began growling. This wasn't his hey-Commodore-I've-got-to-pee growl. This was deeper, lengthier, and far more ominous.

"What's gotten into you, Pep?" he said.

Bob turned his head from the dog to the dune, trying to identify whatever was the focus of his alert. If there was movement, Bob missed it. If there was a shadow, he didn't see it. He wondered if it was possible his feelings about the dune had somehow transferred to the dog. Or maybe it was Pepper who was influencing *him*.

"Maybe we're both just getting too old for..."

He stopped mid-sentence. While continuing to stare into the dune, Pepper took a step back, switched from a growl to a whimper, and peed on the balcony's outdoor carpet. The dog then looked up at Bob and moved quickly to the sliding glass door, whimpering the entire time.

"Yeah, okay, buddy. It was an accident. Something spooked you. You're a good dog."

Bob slid open the door to let Pepper into the condo. He returned with a pitcher of water to rinse the area where the dog peed. Carpet cleaner would have to wait for later. Bob did not want to break eye contact with the dune for any length of time. He returned to the railing, where he remained until the sun began to set behind the span of the Chesapeake Bay Bridge-Tunnel closest to the Virginia Beach shoreline.

A handful of people had now gathered on the beach, taking photos with the setting sun in the background. Bob saw them, knew they were talking and laughing, but had no interest in what they were doing. He stared purposefully out from the balcony—at the Bay, at the beach, at the people, and always back to the dune. The experience with Pepper rattled him.

He was trying to settle down and refocus on the dune when, without warning, Pepper's loud barking from inside got Bob to turn and look into his unit. As soon as Bob entered the condo, he realized Pepper was reacting to someone at the front door. He could distinguish the shadow of a person through the door's smoked glass panel. As he got closer, he could hear Mary Castalano attempting to calm Pepper. Knowing who was on the other side may have eased the dog's anxiety, but it also caused him to bark with more excitement.

"Okay. Okay. It's all right," Bob said.

Pepper immediately began greeting Mary when Bob opened the door. Mary bent to Pepper's level, petting him and telling him how good he was and how much she missed him.

"I thought that was you and Tony on the beach, but I wasn't sure until I heard your voice. I couldn't make out what you were saying, but I recognized your mellow tones. Did you just get back?" Bob asked as they hugged.

"No. We got back yesterday. Split the drive over two days. We took our time and stopped for dinner. I guess we didn't get here until 8:00 p.m. or so."

"Well, it's good to have you back, but, Mary, don't tell me the only reason you came to my door was to convene the latest session of the Mary and Pepper Mutual Admiration Society. Come in for a few minutes. Where's my paisano?"

"That would be reason enough, of course. Right,

Pepper? But I'm also here to invite you and your little friend here for dinner. Nothing fancy. I'm only making spaghetti and meatballs, but there's plenty."

"Gee, Mary, that's really thoughtful of you, but I've got a ton of things to…"

"Oh, that's baloney and you know it, Bob. We will expect the exalted Commodore and his gorgeous little dog at our place in thirty minutes. I already have the water on and the meatballs are in the sauce," she cut him off.

"I know better than to argue with you. I'll take his nibs for a walk and be there in a half hour or so," Bob said.

"In 'a half hour,' it's *al dente*. In 'or so,' it's mush and Mary Castalano does not serve mush. I know there isn't an Italian bone in your German body, but you were assigned to Sigonella once, right? See you in thirty—make that twenty-five minutes."

"Yes, Drill Sergeant." Bob could think of no more appropriate response.

"I love you, Bobby. It's good to see you," she said as she walked away.

"I really am happy you guys are back."

6

"I was going to get flowers and a bottle of better wine, but I was afraid Mary would remove one of my vital organs if I wasn't on time," Bob said to Tony, handing him the bottle. "I had this bottle of red in the house."

"You didn't have to bring anything. We're glad you agreed to come for dinner. It's good to see you again," Tony said.

"I actually have a ton of things to do, but I wasn't given a choice by your dear wife."

"I heard that, Commodore. Bring the flowers into the kitchen. I'll put them in some water." Mary's voice came from the kitchen.

"No, Mary, I didn't bring…"

Mary poked her head out of the kitchen.

"What? No flowers?" Her sly smile betrayed the fact she heard the entire exchange at the door and knew from the start that Bob had not brought flowers. "I'm just giving you a hard time, Commodore."

"How many years have we known each other?" Bob asked, not expecting an answer. "And how many times have I asked you to stop calling me Commodore?"

"I do it because I know it gets the blood circulating through that ancient body of yours, Bob. Tony and I consider it a privilege to know you. You're almost naval royalty, in our opinion," she said.

"Hardly. But I've always said you guys make me feel like family. Only family would treat an old man with such open hostility," Bob said with a chuckle.

"And love you no matter what," Mary added, as she walked out of the kitchen to hug Bob and kiss him on the cheek. "You two start on a glass of wine in the living room. Dinner is still a few minutes off."

"Won't it be mush by then?" Bob said.

"Not a chance. Do you think I was really going to throw the pasta in before you got here? This girl isn't dumb, you know."

"Once again," Bob said. "All I can say is, *yes, Drill Sergeant.*"

Tony handed Bob one of the two glasses of wine he carried into the living room. Pepper abandoned his owner, choosing instead to be with Mary in the kitchen.

"Mary, if the dog gets in your way, just say the word and I'll get him out of there." The condo's open floor plan allowed Bob to talk to Mary from the living room almost without raising his voice.

"Are you kidding?" she said. "We're having a great time in here. It's the first time today I've been able to have an intelligent conversation with a male."

"Oh, man! You walked right into that one, Bob," Tony said. "I think you lost your edge while we were gone."

"Maybe," he said, "but I figure since she's been talking to you all day, I'm in the clear."

"Touché, my friend," Tony said. "Sit. Take a load off."

"Would you mind if we went out on the lanai?" Bob asked.

"Sorry, your naval majesty, but we don't have a lanai in this humble abode. We have a lowly balcony. We can go out there, but I'm coming in if the bugs start biting."

"Nah. Too early for mosquitoes and I don't think the

flies will be biting this year. They were bad last summer. For some reason, they seem to alternate each year," Bob said. "Probably Mother Nature's way of screwing with us."

"I hope you're right. Those biting flies are the worst. They hurt like a son-of-a-bitch."

Bob had moved to the railing and was looking out into the Bay as it slowly surrendered to the evening's darkness.

"It's going to be a clear night. The moon'll light up the beach tonight," Bob said.

"It's a million dollar view," Tony said. He joined Bob at the railing. "Hey, are you okay?"

"What? Yeah, of course. Why do you ask?"

"I didn't want to say anything when you walked in, but you look like shit."

"Thanks, Tony. I love you, too," Bob said. "It isn't easy to look good when I'm standing in the shadow of your stunning self."

"Seriously, you look like you haven't slept in a week. When I looked at you just now, you looked…I don't know…you looked really worried," Tony said.

Bob sipped his wine. "This isn't the wine I brought, is it?"

"That swill? Not a chance. I'll use that to strip paint off the walls. This is the good stuff."

"It does taste good."

"There's plenty."

"Oh, no. I've got to go slow or I'll fall asleep at the table. It hasn't been a week, but it has been a couple of days," Bob said.

"A couple of days for what?" Tony wasn't following Bob's dialogue.

"Since I've slept. Well, that's not true. I nodded off on the lanai the other night. Last night, I think. It all runs together. Anyway, not exactly quality sleep."

"On your balcony?" Tony said. "Did you have too much to drink?"

"No. Hardly touch the stuff anymore. Nah. It's a... it's.... You know, I never realized how hard it would be to explain this to someone."

"Okay," Tony said. "Let me start. Are you dying?"

"Aren't we all? But to answer the question I think you're asking, no, I'm not dying."

"Are you sick?"

"No, Tony. It's nothing like that."

"Well, then, what in the hell is going on? Why aren't you sleeping?"

The door to the balcony opened.

"Are there really still girls on the beach at this hour? If you two dirty old men can put your tongues back in your mouths, please come in for dinner," Mary said.

"To be continued," Tony turned and said quietly to Bob as they walked to the dining room.

"Good Lord, Mary," Bob said. "You cooked enough food for the fleet. Do you think I haven't eaten at all since you two went to Florida for the winter?"

"You may have eaten, but it doesn't look like you've been sleeping," Mary said. "There are dark circles under your eyes."

"And the Bay Ridge Condominium Association award for Miss Subtle of the Century goes to my wife," Tony said, extending his arm in Mary's direction.

"Oh, Tony, Bob knows me well enough to know I'm direct with the people I care about most."

"That's true," Bob said.

"And, by the way, I intentionally made an extra pound of pasta so there would be enough for you to take home for a meal or two and for us to have leftovers, as well," Mary said. "Now, to return to my point, are you feeling okay? I'm worried about you. I don't like the way you look."

"Yeah. I feel fine, but, you're right. I haven't slept well the last night or so."

"All right, instead of coffee, have another glass of wine with dessert. It'll help you sleep."

"Yes, mother," Bob said.

"At least he didn't call you Drill Sergeant again," Tony said.

Dinner continued with a mix of general conversation and banter. Bob hadn't enjoyed himself this much in a very long time. Not surprisingly, he followed Mary's direction by having wine with his piece of apple pie.

"Well, that was a great dinner, Mary. And you're right, I think I'm going to sleep well tonight."

"Maybe I'll stop by tomorrow for a cup of coffee," Tony said to Bob.

"Anytime. I should be home all day."

"Mary is going to an early lunch to catch up on the news and the rumors with the girls in the neighborhood. I'll stop by late morning or early afternoon."

"And if you arrive hungry, I have some leftover spaghetti with meatballs," Bob said, motioning to the containers he was carrying home.

"I snuck in the leftover apple pie, as well," Mary said.

"Wait. You gave him my pie?" Tony asked.

"Yes. And Bob, don't you dare share your food with Tony. We have plenty here," Mary said. She kissed Bob on the cheek. "Good night, my Commodore. Get some sleep."

"Thanks again for dinner. Let's go, Pepper."

Bob and the dog rode the elevator up one floor. After he put the food in his refrigerator, he put Pepper on his leash. Back down in the elevator for a quick walk to close out the night.

He tossed the dog a treat when they returned to the condo. Bob walked toward the sliding glass door, but stopped when he got to the middle of the living room.

"You know, Pepper, I think I'm too tired to spend any more time on the lanai. I've given the dune enough attention for now. The last thing I need is another crappy night's sleep outside in a chair. The boogie man is just going to have to wait another day if he wants to attack me out there."

Bob moved to his bedroom, stripped off his clothes, and climbed into bed. He was asleep in minutes.

*There is constant struggle
between good and evil in the world.
It is up to good people to choose the right side.*

Nelson Mandela

Wednesday

7

"I didn't expect to see you this early," Bob said when he walked from the balcony to open the front door. He hadn't actually heard the doorbell, but Pepper did and that was enough to get Bob's attention.

"Do you want me to come back later? Don't tell me the old Commodore has a little honey in his bedroom. Did you get lucky last night? It's always the quiet ones who get the action. Don't you want her to meet your old friend, Tony? I understand. I'll just go on home. Your secret is safe with me." Tony actually moved from Bob's front door, as though he was going to return to the elevator.

"Would you shut up?" Bob said, acknowledging that his friend was joking. "That'll be the day. At my age, I only go out after dark to keep my dog from peeing on the carpet."

"Seriously, if it's too early…"

"No. No. It's not too early. You said you'd be by in the late morning or early afternoon is all."

"Yeah, well, I lied. Mary's going to lunch with her girlfriends, but they left early to work up an appetite."

"Got it. That's a euphemism for *they went shopping and will stop for lunch*," Bob said.

"You're partly right. They won't actually stop. I'm guessing they'll only break for lunch and then get right back to the shopping. You know—to work up an appetite for dinner."

By this time, they had walked into the kitchen. Tony and Pepper had finished greeting each other.

"Mind if I make myself a cup of coffee?" Tony asked.

"Help yourself. I'm about ready for a second cup. By the way, the wine did the trick. I slept like a log last night. Had a weird dream that I haven't pieced together yet, but I slept through the night. Don't even remember getting up to use the head."

"Now, that's saying something," Tony said. "Unless you wet the bed, of course. And may I add that I love it when you use military lingo. Real men don't go to the bathroom: they use the head."

"No. No. My sheets were dry, thank you very much. But you're not kidding. It would be saying something if I didn't have to get up at least once at night. And, may I add regarding my use of Navy terminology for the bathroom— you're an idiot."

They both smiled, silently acknowledging how much they enjoyed poking fun at each other. Mary often expressed her amazement at how Bob and Tony seldom missed the opportunity to take rhetorical swipes at each other, without either one ever being offended. Whenever she said something about it, Tony would remind her that women just don't interact that way.

"But you were okay when you woke up?" Tony asked.

"Absolutely. I woke up early and refreshed. So far, I've just been sitting on the lanai."

"You know, I should have gone out to get doughnuts or something. Not much of a visitor, am I?" Tony said, looking around the kitchen.

"Why? Because you didn't bring any food or because you always show up hungry?"

"Jesus, you *do* know me, don't you?"

"Have a piece of the pie you guys sent home with me last night. God knows I don't need the calories."

"You know, I think I will. Can I cut a piece for you?"

"No, not for me," Bob said. "I already ate breakfast. I'll have a piece later on."

"If I decide to leave any for you," Tony said.

"I'll tell your wife if you don't."

"You win. There will be plenty here when you decide to have some. You don't play fair. Do you know that, Bob?"

They walked onto Bob's balcony. Tony carried his coffee and a large piece of last night's dessert. He also had the undivided attention of Pepper, who was ready to consume any crumb that fell off Tony's plate. Sitting up on his hind legs, the dog begged for Tony to be overly generous.

"Like I said to you last night, Bob, this is a million dollar view. Whoa! And here comes a school of dolphins," Tony said.

"Jeez, you're a regular Jacques Cousteau, aren't you? It isn't a school of dolphins, Tony, it's a pod," Bob said.

"Pod…schmod…who cares? They're still great to watch."

Tony sat at the high table, looking through the binoculars Bob always kept there. Bob opted to stand on the other side of the table. They both looked out silently for a minute or two, watching the dolphins swim from west to east, where the Bay meets the ocean.

"Want to use the binoculars?" Tony asked, extending them to Bob.

"No. They're close enough this morning," Bob said.

"Okay. So what is it you couldn't tell me last night because we were summoned to the dinner table?" Tony said.

"You know, I've been trying to come up with the best way to begin this conversation and not sound like a nut case in the process."

"Why don't you just jump in?"

"No. Let me ask you a question first. In all the years you've owned a place here, you've heard stories about the dune, haven't you?"

"I don't know what you mean by stories. Carol and Bo Walsh have told Mary and me about some of the stray animals they've seen from their balcony. Excuse me, Commodore, from their lanai. They've talked about how far into the dune the Bay has come during some storms. And we all know how much Bo hates it when some A-hole walks around in the dune. Is that what you mean?"

"Bo's right. It's against the law. More important, though, it's real easy to damage the dune, but I'll spare you my usual lecture," Bob said.

"Thank you, Oh, Commodore, My Commodore," Tony replied, bowing in a show of mock respect.

"But that's not what I'm talking about," Bob said, ignoring Tony's gesture. "I'm talking about mysterious things. Haven't you ever heard any stories about the dune that are hard to explain?"

"Oh, are you talking about the bullshit stories? That's what I call them. You know, the kind kids tell at summer camp? I suppose I've heard some of those, but I can't remember any specifically. Frankly, I don't put a lot of stock in ghost stories, Bob."

"Yeah, well…," Bob began. "So, I guess you don't like the story of the hotel clerk who was killed here on the property."

"And whose ghost still haunts the place? No. Sorry. Great story for around the campfire, Ke-mo sah-bee, but not something I think about seriously," Tony said. "Oh, I'm sure the poor guy bought it that night, but I don't subscribe to the ghost part. Now, I do remember, at one of our community cookouts by the pool—Memorial Day or Fourth of July, I think—a few old timers were trading stories about the Navy SEALs conducting war games in the dune. Hell, you might have been one of them," Tony said.

"Wasn't me. I've heard those stories about the SEALs. They're BS, for sure. The SEALs are based at Little Creek, just to the west. Sure, they routinely cross this part of the Bay to conduct drills and exercises over there (he pointed to the east) on Fort Story. There is absolutely no reason why they would use our dune when they have those two military installations so close. Plus, there are so many other Navy, Army, and even Air Force locations for them to pick from in the Tidewater region. Nah, those stories are just from a group of old farts who want the Navy to pay for beach reclamation. It's all baloney," Bob said.

"Well, that's what I remember being told. I never saw them, of course."

"No. And you won't because…"

"Because they're Ninjas," Tony finished the sentence.

"Funny. No. Because they don't train in our dune and that's just a fact," Bob said. "The stories I'm talking about are unexplained or unsolved."

"Like what?" Tony asked.

"Jeez. There are a ton about our dune and this area. And I bet even I don't know the half of them," Bob said.

"Let me guess. And you are now going to tell me some," Tony said.

"Well, I'm glad you asked, my friend. I'm happy to share a taste of our local history."

"Here we go," Tony said.

"Back in the late '60s or early '70s, a sailor who just got back from duty off the coast of Vietnam, comes home to an empty apartment. His wife ran off with some guy and left him high and dry. She left an awful 'Dear John' letter on their kitchen counter. The young man parks his car right out here on Page Avenue and walks out onto the beach with a couple of six-packs and a bottle of Jack Daniels. After eight beers and a third of the bottle of Jack, he wanders into the dune probably to pee, or puke, or both."

Bob looked directly into Tony's eyes to be sure he was paying attention.

"Go on. I'm listening," Tony said.

"Well, he was considered UA by the Navy the next day—that's an unauthorized absence—and declared a deserter thirty days later.

"That sucks, but I bet that happened a lot during the war," Tony said.

"Sure, but this guy was no deserter. Petty Officer S.T. Pettiford was a model sailor who was trying to drown his sorrows. I know. The young man was a shipmate of mine," Bob said.

"So, what do *you* think happened? Although, I'm pretty sure I know what's coming."

"The police found four unopened beers and what was left of the Jack Daniels at the edge of the dune. They also found a canvas bag that had S.T.'s wallet, car keys, and a few personal items."

"But no sign of him?" Tony said.

"That's exactly what the police said. They said he was gone. No sign of foul play. So, the Navy drew a conclusion that didn't do justice to a good sailor."

"That had to be tough for you, and for his family."

"Still is. Believe me."

"Look, Bob. I'll grant you that is a strange story about an unexplained disappearance, but there was so much going on in that kid's life. I have to believe he found a way to commit suicide and have the body not be found. I don't know how he did it. Maybe animals got to his body before the police could find it."

"Animals? You're nuttier than me, Tony. Animals? Do you think there are tigers or lions in the dune, going unnoticed as they eat people? Seriously?"

"Well, I suppose there could be a lot of reasonable explanations. I just can't sign up for something supernatural. Sorry."

"No need to apologize to me. That's not the only unexplained disappearance, as you call it. There are other stories about kids who disappeared in the dune. Police come up with rationalizations that involve drinking and drowning…"

"But you don't buy it?"

"Can't. Not in every case. Every few years, there's another disappearance. Sometimes, they know the kids were on our beach. Sometimes they have no idea. Sometimes, they find a beer can or two."

"Big deal. It's not hard to find a beer can in the dune."

"Exactly, but you know what, Tony? In almost fifty years, they've never acknowledged finding a body. Not in the dune or washed ashore somewhere along the coast. That's just not normal. There's no way a body was not found in any of these cases. No way."

"So, you think some government agency has a collection of dead bodies somewhere?" Tony pressed him.

"I'm not saying that. But, what if the bodies they did find were mutilated or killed in such a way that they didn't want to share the details with the public?"

"And why would they do that?"

"Come on, Tony. The police routinely withhold certain pieces of information about a murder scene. That way, they can determine if they're dealing with a serial killer, a copy cat, or a series of random acts."

"Bob, if you're right, your serial killer is probably ninety years old by now," Tony said, with a small tone of ridicule in his voice.

"I know. I'm having trouble with that part of my theory."

"Look, I'm not saying all these things can be explained…"

"Right," Bob interrupted. "What about the classic story linked to the Ash Wednesday storm in the early sixties? That's the last one I know of where there is any mention of a body."

"Oh, I know that one and I think it gets blown more and more out of proportion every time it's retold."

"I don't know about that. I first heard it twenty or twenty-five years ago and it hasn't changed at all. Not when I tell it."

"C'mon, Bob. Bodies with no skeletons or internal organs, disintegrating when the sailors try to pull them out of the water. I don't know."

"How do we know if some of these other cases, where they claim no body was recovered, weren't similar situations?" Bob asked.

"Now you're going conspiracy theory on me. I think you're stretching believability to the breaking point, Bob."

"Of course, the Navy agrees with you, Tony. The Navy says it never happened."

"Probably because it never did," Tony said.

"We'll never know. Will we? But you're a good Catholic boy, Tony. Do you know what the priest says on Ash Wednesday?" Bob said.

"He probably starts with, 'Good morning. What's for breakfast?'"

"Smart ass. I'm talking about when he puts ashes on your forehead?"

"No. It's been years. What does he say?"

"Remember you are dust and unto dust you shall return. That's what he says. Makes you wonder. Certainly makes me wonder," Bob said.

"Bob, what the hell has gotten into you? Since when are you the kind of person who falls for these bizarre stories," Tony said. "Tell me. Were you visited by little green men? Did they take you to their leader? Wait! Did they use probes on that wrinkled old prune of a body of yours?"

"No, but that brings me to what I started to explain last night, before dinner," Bob said, in a rare instance of ignoring the sarcasm. "I thought these stories would be a good intro, but I guess I was wrong." Bob put his coffee cup on the table and walked slowly to the balcony's railing. He looked down at the dune. "Tony, I can't explain this very well, but I'm convinced something bad is going on in the dune. I know it sounds crazy, but I've had this feeling. I've tried to get it out of my mind, but it's no use. There's something in there and it...it..."

"Hey, you're not kidding, are you? Has something happened? What did you see that makes you think something is wrong?" Tony said.

"You better believe I'm not kidding. Look, for a thousand years, sailors have told tales about the dunes they've encountered when they come ashore. But I'm telling you, this is different. I've had a very real uneasiness about our dune for the last few days. I'll be honest with you, I was relieved when I saw that you and Mary were back. I figured I might be able to get my mind off of the damn dune, but I haven't been able to. Tony, it's scaring the shit out of me."

"Maybe it's some kind of bug. Have you seen a doctor? Could you be dehydrated?" Tony had joined Bob at the railing. His concern for his friend was genuine, but he was at a loss for what to do.

"No. This is no bug. Dehydrated? That's almost funny, Tony," Bob responded. "I'm drinking water or tea all day long and I'm pissing crystal clear before noon every day. I am certainly not dehydrated."

"Well, that's certainly a lot more information than I needed to know," Tony said.

"Hey, you asked, Paisano. I really do appreciate your concern, Tony, but I'm sure what I'm feeling has to do with the dune and not with my hydration. The other day, I met this young girl who was walking in the dune."

"Really? A young girl?"

"Yeah. I told her it was against the law to walk in the dune and that kicked off a very pleasant conversation." Bob was yet to take his eyes off the dune.

"Okay," Tony said, drawing out his pronunciation of the word. "How long did you talk to her?"

"Oh, not long. She had to get home to study for an exam. But I gave her a kind of homework assignment. I told her to learn more about dunes—the stories about them, and specifically, what Marco Polo has to say about them," Bob continued.

"Marco Polo?"

"Right. The explorer."

"And have you seen her again?"

"Sure. She was here yesterday. She's as smart as a whip. She found out a good bit about Marco Polo and we talked about the dangers and mystery surrounding dunes. I told her a few of the stories I shared with you."

"You didn't."

"Yeah, I did. One of my worries is that I made the dunes sound more exciting than dangerous. That's part of my dilemma. I guess I'm worried about her, as well." Bob finally turned his head. He read the look on Tony's face. "You think I'm full of crap, don't you? You don't believe a word I'm saying."

"Bob, that's not it. I believe you think you saw this mysterious girl emerge from the dune. I do. I just…"

"Emerge from the dune? What the hell are you talking about? I never said anything about her *emerging* from the dune. And she's not all that mysterious. She's just a kid who goes to Cox High School down on North Great Neck Road, for God's sake. I expect she'll be back in the next day or so."

"I can't wait to meet her," Tony said, but the insincerity in his voice came through loud and clear.

"Oh, screw you. Once again, you're lucky I love you like a brother or I'd toss your sorry ass off the lanai and into the dune."

"Oh, please, Commodore, don't throw me to the demons in the dune. Please." Tony feigned fear in his voice as he got down on one knee.

"Okay, I'm changing the subject." Bob was annoyed Tony was not more accepting, but he liked him too much to be angry. He returned to the table to take a drink from his coffee cup. "You think I'm a lonely old man who's getting a little nutty. And now I make up stories and I even have an imaginary friend."

Tony stayed at the railing, looking out at the dune and the Bay.

"Look, Bob, I don't think you're crazy. I could be convinced you're a little lonely. If you say you met this high school kid who was walking in the dune, I'll go along with it. But I am worried about the, the—I don't know—the anxiety you're having over what might happen in the dune. That's just not normal, my friend. I think maybe you should see somebody about that."

67

"So, you *do* think I'm going crazy. Is that really what you're saying?"

"Bob. Bob. If I looked at the dune long enough, I could probably convince myself there is mystery in there. Especially if I was having trouble sleeping," Tony said.

"I'm not worried about the dune because I'm having trouble sleeping. I'm having trouble sleeping because I'm worried about the dune," Bob said.

"No, I get it. But, you know, I can look out at the dune—especially at night with a full moon—and imagine something behind that clump of dune grass there." Tony pointed into the dune. "Or that one there." He shifted, indicating another area. "Hell, or even in that opening right there. That would be a great place for something to…"

Tony stopped because Bob had rejoined him at the railing and had a firm grip on his arm.

"Opening? What are you talking about?" Bob asked.

"Right there. Directly in front of us. Right there in that small clearing in the dune grass. Can't you see it?" Tony said. "It looks like the mouth of a miniature mine shaft right there in the dune. If I let my imagination go wild, I could spin a yarn about it myself."

"Oh, my God," Bob said.

"What? It's just a hole in a mound of sand, Bob."

"The hell it is," Bob said. "It wasn't there yesterday and it wasn't there this morning."

"Bob, it's a hole. An opening in the sand, for God's sake. You're acting as though it's the gateway to hell," Tony said.

"Look at the opening closely, Tony. It's too big to have been made by a rabbit, or a raccoon, or a skunk."

"I'm not so sure about that, but even if you're right, you know as well as I do that there are fox and coyote in the state park right down the beach between here and Fort

Story. What's to say a fox hasn't wandered onto the dune for a little privacy? And I still think it's only big enough for a rabbit warren," Tony countered.

"The opening is very well formed. It's as though it's been there for a while."

"So what if it has?"

"You're not listening to me, Tony," Bob said. "That opening wasn't there when you rang my doorbell. It wasn't there when I walked off this lanai to open the front door. But look. Look at it. It doesn't look as though it was just dug. It looks like it's been there a while."

It would be wrong to describe the urgency in Bob's voice as panic, but his increased level of concern was clear.

"Okay. Okay," Tony said. "If you say it wasn't there an hour ago, I'm not going to argue with you. It wasn't there. But you have to admit you're not exactly intimately familiar with every feature of the dune."

"A week ago that would have been a true statement, but the last few days I think I've studied every inch of the damn dune—at least the area directly behind our building. I'm serious when I tell you the opening out there was formed since you walked into my condo." Bob wanted to leave no doubt of his sincerity in Tony's mind. He was also conscious of the fact that Tony might now seriously consider him mentally or emotionally unstable.

They both stood looking out from the balcony. Bob was singularly focused on the opening in the dune. Tony's eyes looked out into the Bay. He was trying to think of something encouraging to say, but he was becoming convinced his friend might be showing signs of reduced mental capacity. He wasn't sure if Bob was beginning to suffer from dementia or if some other medical condition was causing him to be delusional. He planned to talk with his wife and maybe the Walshes, hoping they would be able to develop a strategy to get Bob to agree to see a doctor.

"How about this," Tony began. "Maybe an animal—a rabbit or maybe even a fox or coyote—tunneled into the dune somewhere farther out or over to the left or the right. What we're looking at could be an exit from an existing tunnel instead of the entrance to something new. That could explain it, right?"

"I suppose. You may be right." Bob decided to imply he accepted Tony's explanation because he knew he wasn't making any headway with him. He also wanted to keep a close eye on the dune and that wouldn't be possible with Tony hanging around. He hoped Tony would get the hint and leave.

A few more minutes of silence followed as they again stared north from the balcony.

"Hey, Bob. What do you say we go for an early lunch? You pick the place. I'll drive. I'll just run downstairs to get my wallet and car keys."

"Nah, Tony. I wish I could but, after last night's feast, I'm not up for a big lunch. Besides, you and Mary gave me all that leftover food. I plan to have some of it later on. Maybe an early dinner. I'm also in the middle of a…"

"Okay, you can stop now. Unlike my wife, I'm willing to take no for an answer. Maybe tomorrow we can go for a burger at that place where we can smoke a cigar after lunch."

"That sounds like a good idea," Bob lied.

"Well, I'm going to see if the Seven-Eleven still has any copies of the newspaper. Our delivery doesn't start until tomorrow," Tony said.

"I'd give you mine, but I haven't read it yet," Bob said as they walked to the front door.

Tony grabbed the knob, but turned to Bob with the door still shut.

"Look," Tony said. "I'm going to say this, but I don't want you to get pissed off or over react. Okay?"

"I'm all ears," Bob said.

"If you ever get a case of the heebie-jeebies because of that damn dune, I want you to promise me you'll give me a call. I can be here in a matter of seconds."

"Thanks, Tony. I appreciate that," Bob said.

"I mean it. If you see anything you don't like. If something makes you uncomfortable, just yell and I'm here. I think I've told you this before, but, in case I haven't, I have a gun in the house."

"Oh, you do?"

"It's totally legal. I even have a conceal carry permit," Tony said.

"That's good to know, but I have no plans to challenge you to a duel."

Tony gave Bob a sideways look and, as he pulled the door open he said, "Now, who's being the asshole?"

They both laughed.

"I'll see you tomorrow, Tony."

After a brief pit stop, Bob returned to the balcony. Pepper sat at the door to the rear stairs, asking to go out.

"I'll be watching you, Pepper. Lift your leg and get right back up here."

Even before Pepper got to the bottom of the stairs, Bob had taken up his position, watching the opening in the dune. A slight movement on the walkway below got his sudden attention. Bob realized that the sensation he just experienced was fear. It lasted only seconds because he saw it was Pepper mooching around on the boardwalk. The dog moved slowly to the edge closest to the dune.

"Pepper, get up here," Bob said the moment he heard

71

the dog's low growl. It was definitely directed into the dune. Pepper turned and ran up the stairs at Bob's command. He reentered the balcony. Bob shut the door without taking his eyes off the hole in the dune—the hole that wasn't there an hour ago.

Bob was uncomfortable with his current situation. He prided himself as an independent-minded man who wasn't afraid to challenge popular opinion. He was The Commodore, for God's sake. But here he was—captive to an opening in a dune on the southern end of the Chesapeake Bay. And for reasons that defied logic, he had just experienced brief, but bone-chilling, fear.

"What the hell is going on?" he said softly. "God and every shipmate I have ever had, who has died and gone to heaven, must be looking down at me, laughing their asses off," he said in a low voice. Pepper looked up as though the comments were directed at him, but, in fact, Bob was talking aloud to himself.

"Can you believe this crap, Pepper?" he said. "Of course, if I keep talking out loud to myself or to you, Tony is going to have me committed for sure."

Pepper tilted his head upward with a facial expression a cynic might describe as a "you-*do*-know-I'm-a-dog" look.

"What in the hell is that?" Bob said, as he reached for the binoculars.

His eyes had shifted up briefly from the dune, when he saw a ship sitting at anchor. It was well out in the Bay, close to the second span of the Bridge-Tunnel. Even before he raised his binoculars, Bob knew he was not looking at a US Navy vessel. It was a civilian ship used to transport coal that arrived by train from the mines in Pennsylvania and West Virginia. From the port in Norfolk, it was transported to any number of countries around the world. He focused the binoculars, briefly studying the ship.

"Now, that's just not right," he said. He might have

looked through the binoculars a lot longer but a voice in his head told him to refocus on the dune. Bob stood for a while with his hands on the railing. He moved a chair from the table, and sat with eyes on the dune and the mysterious opening.

"I knew I would find you still standing guard over that damn hole."

Tony stood on the narrow boardwalk, off to Bob's left. He had a newspaper under his arm and a Styrofoam cup of coffee in one hand. He had walked from the parking lot and across the pool deck to get there.

"Checking up on me?" Bob asked.

"Actually, I crossed the pool deck because I wanted to get a closer look at the hole and I figured you'd still be on duty, waiting for God knows what to emerge."

"You joke," Bob said.

Tony walked slowly along the boardwalk until he was aligned with the opening in the dune. He stood up on his toes and stretched his neck to see as much of it as possible from that angle.

"The dune grass is a lot taller than I ever realized," Tony said. "It's taller than I am. You really have a better view from your balcony—I mean your lanai. But I can see the hole by looking through the grass from here, and I'll be damned if I didn't have it right. It does look like a miniature mine entrance. Do you see what I mean? It's kind of rounded at the top. Almost like a slice from a loaf of bread. "

"Yeah, I see what you mean. Hey, Tony, what do you make of that ship out there?" Bob said, pointing toward the coaler.

"The what?" He followed the direction of Bob's arm. "I can't really see from here. I'm at a bad angle and the dune grass is too high. What is it?"

"It's a coaler and it wasn't there this morning," Bob said.

"Oh, so that just appeared, too?" Tony looked up at Bob, but didn't wait for an answer. "Did you check it out with your binoculars?"

"I did. It's a coaler all right. It must have moved in when I was focused on the dune."

Tony did not want to revisit the subject of unexplained appearances. Instead he said, "I thought the Navy ran all of them out of this part of the Bay a year or more ago because they obstruct Navy access to the Atlantic from Norfolk."

"You're exactly right. A few years ago, you'd see more than a dozen of those rust buckets sitting out there waiting to be called in to get loaded with coal. Nobody cared when we complained about what they did to the view or how they polluted the water, but the Navy finally noticed and ran their asses way out into the Bay to sit and wait."

"Maybe she's got a rookie captain who hasn't gotten the word about where to wait for the call to move to the harbor," Tony said.

"Not a chance," Bob answered. "Captains of ships like that may not be the most celebrated men, but they are not stupid. Besides, there's no way any ship could get as close as it is without the pilots knowing about it. I can tell from here that ship is sitting way too low in the water to be empty. It's full for sure."

"Well, my favorite Commodore of the high seas, why do *you* think it's there?" Tony said.

"Could be engine trouble, I suppose. Whatever it is, I bet a pilot boat or the Coast Guard pays it a visit before too long," Bob said. "Not to change the subject, but I'm thinking I got you hooked on the mystery of the dune and that's why you couldn't resist using the boardwalk instead of your front door."

"Not really. Like I said, I just wanted to get a closer look at what has captivated my crazy old neighbor. I may have to give a statement to the mental health people when they come to take you away."

"If I had a bucket of warm piss up here, my dear friend, I'd dump it on you for that remark," Bob said.

After smiling and waving off Bob's comment, Tony walked further along the boardwalk. Shortly before it ended, he turned right to walk up the set of exterior stairs that led to his and the other five condos' balconies at that end of the building.

Resuming his position at the railing, now to observe both the dune and the newly arrived coaler out in the Bay, Bob turned his comments to his dog.

"What do you think, Pepper? Am I just a crazy old man?" Bob put the binoculars to his eyes. "Smart dog. Not ready to comment either way. I'll tell you what, old dog, I don't like that ship and I don't like whatever is going on in the dune."

Pepper issued another low growl.

"So, you don't like it either? I guess I'm just going to have to do something about it before too long."

8

Bob stayed at the railing nearly all of the remainder of the day. He took occasional short breaks to use the bathroom or to refresh his drink, but that was it. After his third cup, he switched from coffee, alternating among iced tea, water, and Diet Pepsi.

Dolphins made another appearance, this time swimming from east to west. Their movement was smooth and graceful, of course, but to Bob they seemed to be swimming much faster than usual.

"What's your hurry, kids?" Bob said to the passing pod. "You're supposed to give me time to admire your movement."

Bob also watched four or five pilot boats move between spans of the Bridge-Tunnel. He was sure they were headed to ships positioned somewhere out in the Bay. The only legal way for a commercial vessel to navigate the Chesapeake Bay was to have a certified Bay pilot on the bridge.

Bob expected one of the pilot boats would stop alongside the lone coaler anchored near the second bridge span. He assumed a Bay pilot would go aboard either to oversee the ship's movement into port or to get it the hell out of these close-in waters. All but one pilot boat passed the coaler as though it wasn't there. He swore it was some kind of optical illusion caused by the reflection of sunlight on the water, but one of the pilot boats appeared to navigate directly through the coaler, from bow to stern.

"Whoa! If that don't beat all. That's a hell of a trick," Bob said aloud.

As had become standard for the week, Bob again lost complete track of time while he surveyed the dune—and now the Bay, as well—looking for any change to the opening or to the position of the coaler. Eventually, he developed a mild headache to go along with a growing emptiness in his stomach. He checked his watch. He hadn't eaten since he had a bowl of cereal before Tony's visit and now it was after 4:00. He had completely abandoned his routine of light snacks in lieu of lunch.

Before going inside, he gave the dune and the Bay one additional close going-over, noting especially the area around the opening. He made a mental record of where the coaler was in relation to the span of the Bridge-Tunnel that served as its background. If anything changed in the dune or the Bay, Bob was confident he would recognize the difference when he returned to the balcony after he ate.

"Hey, kiddo," Bob said to Pepper. "Let's go in and get an early dinner."

Pepper reacted with a look that said, *I thought you'd never ask.*

Bob heated a generous portion of last night's leftovers in the microwave. Tony's obvious concern for Bob's well-being was on his mind as he ate. He decided not to rush through his meal. He would sit at the dining room table with his food and a Diet Pepsi. He turned on the television just loud enough so he could hear it from the dining room.

Bob thumbed through the newspaper as he ate, all the while with CNN in the background.

When he was done with his meal, Bob used the bathroom and then took Pepper out the front door for a walk. Still remembering Tony's concern, he was determined to give Pepper an unhurried walk. The dog loved it.

The beach has been there for thousands of years at least, and the dune for almost as long, he told himself. *Whatever score it has to settle with me will happen, but I can't let it control my life.*

As much as Bob meant it, he couldn't help thinking about the dune throughout his walk with Pepper. The appearance of the opening had him on edge. And he wanted to know what, if anything, the coaler had to do with the situation.

Bob and Pepper returned to the condo almost precisely at six o'clock. Pepper munched on a treat while Bob washed his hands. He used the remote to switch to the local NBC affiliate for a bit of news focused on Norfolk, Virginia Beach, and the surrounding area. The overly animated meteorologist told him it would be a mostly clear night with the ever-present chance of a pop-up thunderstorm. Rain chances increased over the next few days, with a 50/50 chance the weekend would be a washout.

"Great. It always rains on the weekend," Bob said aloud to himself.

He poured a tall glass of iced tea and walked to the back door. He left the television on, as he did most afternoons. Between 5:00 and 7:00, there was a mix of local and national news. Any time he came back in from the balcony, he would pick up snippets of a story or two. If something caught his attention, he might pause. He considered it a very effective way to stay informed while getting the most of the view. He hadn't found much enjoyment relaxing on the balcony this week and wondered if he would ever be able to sit out there again, mindlessly enjoying the Bay, the dolphins, and the dune.

"Well, Mr. Pepper. Are you ready to go back to work?"

The dog preceded Bob out the sliding door. Bob took a sip of his iced tea and placed the glass on the table. He picked up the binoculars and turned toward the railing.

"Son of a…"

Bob stopped in mid-sentence as he took the few steps

needed to get to the railing. He trained the binoculars on the opening in the dune. There were unmistakable signs of activity at its outer edge. The opening remained well formed, but Bob could see the sand at its mouth was no longer smooth. What looked almost like a rumpled, off-white welcome mat when his eyes were unaided by binoculars, now showed clearly as several long feathers. Some white. Some gray.

"Something either came in or went out of the damn thing. Looks like a sea bird might have gotten a bit too close. There might have been a struggle. And I missed it. Shit!"

Bob moved the binoculars left and right. He looked in vain for a pattern of foot, paw, or talon prints moving to or from the opening.

"Something happened while we were gone, Pepper. Whatever it is inside that damn hole, it knew I wasn't here. Either it's mocking me or it's daring me to engage it."

Bob took the binoculars from his eyes so he could get a wider view of the dune. He looked left and right again. He saw no movement in the dune other than the slight sway of the dune grass in the gentle breeze.

"Nothing to see," he said. "Damn."

Bob moved the binoculars to his eyes again, this time to check out the coaler.

"What in the name of…"

He swept the binoculars side to side and then pulled them from his eyes to get a wider view of the Bay.

A bright light appeared on the bridge of the coaler. It reminded Bob of a camera flash. It lasted only a second or two, but grew in intensity until it whited out Bob's view of the ship. When the light faded, the coaler was gone.

9

"Tony, it's Bob."

"Yeah, I know. I saw it on the caller ID, but I answered anyway. What's up?"

"Have you been watching the Bay?"

"Aren't you going to call me a smart ass?" Tony asked.

"Have you been watching the Bay?" Bob repeated, ignoring his friend's comment.

"Well, every now and then, I look out the window, but I can't say I've been religious about it. Why? Is something wrong? Did something crawl out of the hole?"

"Maybe. I can't be sure. I went inside to get a bite to eat. Then I took the dog for a short walk. When I got back out here…"

"The hole was covered up?" Tony tried to finish Bob's sentence.

"No, but it looks like there was activity of some kind outside the opening and the…"

"Bob. Bob, you've got to give it a rest. Seriously."

"That's not the half of it. I was inside for only a few minutes. When I came back out, I saw the coaler light up like the sun. And now it's gone."

"That's nuts. I didn't understand where you were pointing when I was on the boardwalk," Tony said. "As soon as I got back up here, I looked out into the Bay, but I didn't see anything out of the ordinary. I guess I missed it. Wait. Did I hear you right? What do you mean, it lit up like the sun?"

"Just what I said. There was a bright light on the bridge. It got brighter. When the light went out, the coaler wasn't there anymore. It's gone, Tony," Bob said. "It isn't as though it sailed away. It's like it disappeared."

"What did you eat, Bob?"

"Why the hell does that matter?"

"Bear with me, okay? What did you have to eat?"

"I had a plate of Mary's spaghetti with a couple of meatballs."

"You reheated a plate of spaghetti. Did you turn on the television and maybe search for a channel?"

"Oh, for God's sake. Yes, the TV was on and I put on the local news. Where is this going, Tony? I'm not kidding about this. It's starting to get to me."

"And I'm willing to bet you poured yourself a drink. And knowing you, Mr. Walnut-sized Bladder, you used the bathroom."

"It was a can of Diet Pepsi and I peed twice, smart ass."

"Now, there's my favorite comeback."

"Your what?" Bob asked.

"Never mind. And you said you took the dog for a walk," Tony said.

"And I took the dog for a walk. Your point?"

"My point is that it sounds as though you were away from the balcony long enough for the coaler to have sailed to Annapolis or grown wings and flown to England. Seriously, Bob, are you all right?"

Tony had a point. There had been more than enough time for the coaler to have started its engines and moved to a location well out of Bob's line of sight. Even if it had been disabled, repairs could have been ongoing the whole time it sat there. The pilot boats that passed might have known it would be moving once repairs were made. There might have already been a pilot aboard to help the ship navigate the Bay. But none of that explained the sudden light.

"Maybe someone on the bridge lit a cigarette and that's what you saw," Tony suggested.

"Maybe you're right, Tony. Maybe I made more of the coaler than I should have," Bob said, but he wasn't ready to give up on his suspicions about the ship.

"Of course, I'm right. Where are you now?"

"I'm on my lanai."

"Bob, get off the damn thing. Go inside. Put your feet up and watch a movie. Let it go, my friend."

"Yeah, okay. Thanks for listening. I'll talk to you later."

After he ended the phone call, Bob pocketed his cell phone and stared out at the Bay. He stood there until the sun began to set, moving only to shift his weight. Despite his renewed vigilance, he saw nothing out of the ordinary in the Bay, on the beach, or in the dune.

Eventually, he went inside. He ate a light snack, since he was still full from his early dinner, walked the dog again, and returned to his recliner where he watched the Washington Nationals lose a close game to the New York Mets. At some point during the post-game show, Bob fell asleep.

He who passively accepts evil is as much involved in it as he who helps perpetuate it. He who accepts evil without protesting against it is really cooperating with it.

Martin Luther King, Jr.

Thursday

10

Bob's own snoring woke him about 2:00 a.m. Thursday.

Great. Asleep in two different chairs in one week, he thought. He was confused about the time. He knew it had to be after midnight, but it took him a minute to recognize that the game between the Nationals and the Mets was being re-aired.

"I think I know how this one ends," Bob said as he stood and walked to the bathroom.

Passing through his bedroom, Bob noticed Pepper curled up on the bedspread.

"Couldn't hang with the old man, Pep?"

Only Pepper's eyes moved as they followed Bob. The dog had called it a night—probably hours ago. Bob walked back through the bedroom and used the remote to turn off the television. He paused before dousing the lamp next to his recliner. He decided to give the dune and the Bay one last look before he went to bed.

The sky was clear and the moonlight strong again tonight. The situation in the dune was no different than when he and Tony were together hours ago. The combination of the natural light from the moon and the single light bulb on each level of the back stairwells of his building produced a forest of shadows in the dune. Bob knew Tony had a point. It wouldn't take much of an imagination to convince himself he was seeing almost anything. Add the movement provided by the night breeze, and anyone's worst fears or highest hopes could become reality.

The more he stared into the dune, the more convinced he became that there was a small red light somewhere deep within the opening. Actually, it wasn't a single light at all. There appeared to be two tiny red dots. There was no way to guess how deep in the opening they might be.

I suppose those could be eyes looking out at me, Bob thought. *Or, it could be two rocks reflecting light in just the right way to annoy me.*

In the event he was being watched by something from within that awful hole, Bob decided to send a message. With both hands, he gave the finger to the opening and anything within it.

At that point, Bob decided he had done enough imagining for one very long day. The opening remained in the dune. That was a fact. Beyond that, he would hold his imagination in check. Shifting his attention to the Bay, he saw clearly the line of lights on the bridge spans of the Bridge-Tunnel, shimmering like a string of pearls. He followed them from the Virginia Beach shoreline, out to the man-made island where one of the two tunnels began. His eyes continued across the darkness to the next bridge span. At this hour, very few cars moved across the bridge. Bob could see two sets of headlights making their way to Virginia Beach. They sparkled like stars, but their movement was in a straight line across the Bay.

He followed the bridge lights, expecting them to eventually stop when the second tunnel's location was reached. Instead, there was an unexpected break in the pattern. It was as though there was a black hole in the Bay. But Bob knew what it meant.

"I'll be a son-of-a-bitch," Bob said in a low voice. He leaned over the balcony railing, into the darkness. He squinted in an effort to make out the object that stood between him and the lights of the bridge span. He didn't have to try very hard. He knew the coaler had returned.

11

When he finally got to bed, Bob had trouble falling asleep. Napping in the recliner proved not to be the smartest thing he could have done and the return of the coaler was unsettling. After an hour of tossing and turning, however, he fell into a surprisingly deep sleep.

Before she and her husband, Jim, went to bed, after watching the late news in their Bay Ridge Condo unit, Joan Mulligan looked outside her front and rear doors for any sign of her cat, Shadow. Most nights, Shadow would be there, ready to come in. Tonight, Shadow apparently decided to stay out all night. Whenever this happened, Joan would find Shadow in the morning, curled up in a chair on the back porch of their first-floor unit.

Not long after midnight, Shadow's stealthy pursuit of a field mouse took him to the mouth of the opening in the dune. Moments thereafter, a bright light appeared on the bridge of the coaler.

It was after 11:00 in the morning when Pepper decided it was about time to wake The Commodore. Initially, Bob tried to hide his face with his pillow and the bed sheet, but the dog's face washing was relentless.

"It's almost noon, boy. Way too late for us to be doing this," Bob said as they stood on the balcony.

This was the routine Bob had of letting Pepper use the back steps every morning for a quick pit stop near the boardwalk. It was already more than four hours later than their normal time. The chance of Pepper being seen by other residents was far greater.

"You're going to get me in trouble for sure," Bob said to Pepper as he opened the door to the back stairs. "Go down there, pee real fast, and get back up here. I promise you a longer walk later."

Pepper willingly cooperated. After relieving himself, the only thing on the dog's mind was eating and that happened back in the condo. In the minute or two he waited for Pepper, Bob scanned the dune and the Bay. Without the contrast of the night's darkness, he could see no red lights in the dune's opening and the coaler was no longer in the Bay.

In view of the hour, Bob decided scrambled eggs and toast would serve as both breakfast and lunch for the day. He forced himself not to rush through the meal. Over the last few days, Bob had no more than scanned the headlines of the daily newspaper. Today, though, as he finished his brunch, he turned the last page of the sports section, finishing the entire paper.

"One more cup of coffee, Pepper, and I've got to get back to work. Today is the day, old buddy. Today is the day I face the beast."

When they walked onto the balcony, Bob had a baseball cap on his head, a cup of coffee in his hand, and binoculars suspended over his shoulder. With the early afternoon sun high in the sky, Bob surveyed the landscape. No real change to the opening in the dune and no coaler in the Bay.

Two small groups of people were on the beach. They were close enough in either direction for Bob to hear their voices, but not so close that he could understand what they were saying.

Three women in their twenties or early thirties were trying to get their toddlers used to the Bay water that licked their feet. The other group—four male and three female college-aged kids—had spread towels on the sand. A Frisbee was being tossed. One of the guys was sitting on a cooler which Bob was willing to bet contained beer. Colleges were already out for the summer, so this was nothing unusual for a June afternoon. The beach would be busier later in the day when the after-work population would add even more people to the beach through sunset. If he was going to act and go unnoticed, the time was now.

Bob placed his binoculars on the table next to his coffee cup.

"Well, my friend," Bob said to Pepper. "I'm leaving you in control of the lanai until I get back." He reached inside the small storage shed at the far end of the balcony and withdrew a five-foot long walking stick. With a moderate degree of self mockery in his voice, Bob turned to Pepper with the walking stick in his left hand and his right fist over his heart.

"As we used to say to the Emperor, way back in ancient Rome, *those who are about to die, salute you.*"

Pepper sat and barked once, as if to acknowledge the salute and command Bob to carry on with his mission.

"You old goofball, you enjoy any kind of attention. Don't you?"

Pepper followed him to the door leading to the back stairs.

"Not this time, buddy. I'm flying solo. You stay here. I will return, but until I do, you are my representative."

The dog sat with its head tilted, staring at Bob.

12

Bob stood on the edge of the narrow boardwalk. He looked up to ensure he was aligned with his balcony. Then, he stretched his neck, hoping to see far enough into the dune to eyeball the opening.

Tony was right, he thought. *The view is much better from the lanai.*

With the aid of the walking stick, Bob stepped carefully off the boardwalk and into the dune. This was not his first time in the dune. At the beginning of each season, Bob regularly assisted other owners who were members of the Bay Ridge Condo Grounds Committee on a gentle sweep through the area collecting empty cans, discarded beer bottles, deflated beach balls, and an occasional beach umbrella that had been tossed or blown. After particularly strong storms, it was often necessary to wander into the dune to retrieve roof shingles and pieces of siding. Each time, his stay was relatively brief and it was clearly done as a service for the community and, most importantly to Bob, for the dune's well-being.

Today was different.

Despite the pleasantness of the day and the routine nature of the activity on the beach, Bob felt as though he was in alien territory—the surface of another planet or worse, a combat zone. He moved slowly into the dune toward the opening. He stopped every few steps to be sure he was still on course and that he had not drawn the attention of anyone on the beach.

He could see only a small portion of the beach from his location. Two men were walking from east to west. They were probably close to the water's edge because Bob could see only their shoulders and heads.

Then, it caught his eye.

It was difficult to get a clear view from the dune, but it was undeniable. The coaler.

"I'll be damned," he said softly. *Better not say that again until I'm out of the dune*, he thought. A slight smile briefly formed on his face.

A few more steps. He was getting very close to the opening, but he stopped again.

"Shadow. Is that you, Shadow?" Looking directly at him through a patch of dune grass, Bob saw the black cat, a reflection of red in its eyes. From its rhinestone collar, he recognized it as the cat belonging to Joan Mulligan.

"Shadow, you need to get on home before…" Bob had taken a few steps in the cat's direction, expecting it to run off. He stopped when he realized the cat's head didn't appear to be joined to a body.

"Oh, Shadow. What happened to you? Your momma's going to be so sad," Bob said softly.

After another step or two, and with the aid of his walking stick, Bob moved enough sand near the animal to see he was wrong. The cat's head had not been severed. Its body was flat as a pancake. There was no skeletal structure. It appeared to be no more than a pelt with the head still attached.

He had seen dog toys that resembled Shadow's current condition. But this was no chew toy. This was Shadow—a family pet—reduced to a hideous state.

Bob considered turning back, but there was no abandoning the quest at this point. He advanced deeper into the dune. He pushed aside some dune grass with the end of his walking stick. He was within two feet of the opening.

It was larger than he thought it would be, based on his perspective from the balcony. Tony had clearly underestimated the size animal that could fit inside. Despite the brightness of the day or, maybe because of it, the opening was black. Darker, Bob thought, than anything he had ever seen. He held out his hand, open palm.

He didn't know if it was his imagination, but he was convinced he could feel heat coming from the opening. It was as though it emitted a cylinder of heated air aimed directly at his face. He moved his head and shoulders slightly in an effort to see more deeply into the hole, but it was useless. Slight changes in his angle to the opening made no difference. The area within the hole was total darkness. When he leaned forward even a little bit, the air felt hotter still.

"Well, I've come this far," Bob said aloud, but to himself. He stepped even closer to the opening and extended the walking stick into the hole. He probed gingerly, fully expecting the stick to be wrenched from his grip, disappearing into the abyss.

When that didn't happen, he withdrew the walking stick. He stood silently, staring into the opening. He wanted to look out into the Bay to see if the coaler was still there, but he lacked the nerve to take his eyes off the opening.

The faint smell of burning wood reached his nostrils. He guessed the college kids might have started a fire on the beach. It wouldn't be the first time a group dug a hole on the beach to build a fire. On more than a few occasions, Bob had called the fire department for this reason. Open fires on the beach were illegal. The fire department always responded promptly and without lights or sirens. This allowed the firefighters to walk onto the beach unannounced and invariably catch the guilty party.

Typically, no one would be arrested or even cited. If

the firefighters judged the offenders to be unaware of the law and to have no ill-intent, they would let them off with a warning and a promise of arrest if they were called back. In nearly every case, people admitted they had not considered how easily the dune could catch fire and how quickly a dune fire could threaten the neighboring houses and condos. The law was meant to protect people from their own carelessness.

What the hell am I doing thinking about calling the fire department? he thought. *I'm about to come face-to-face with God knows what and I'm concerned with my civic duty. Concentrate, you old fool. Concentrate.*

He took a deep breath, and, acting on an invisible stimulus, Bob quickly stepped forward. Using the walking stick and his feet, he began pushing sand into the opening. His sense of danger grew and he moved his feet more quickly when he became convinced he saw the two red dots appear within the closing hole behind the growing mound of sand. Since he had no idea how deeply into the dune the opening extended, his goal was only to close the opening, not fill the hole.

Faster, damn it. Faster!

He pushed furiously until the opening was gone. When he stopped, he took a step back, but remained focused. His breathing was heavy. His tee shirt and his baseball cap were soaked with sweat.

Bob waited. He stared at the site where the opening had been. He squinted. His eyes were nearly closed, but not because of the glare. It was in anticipation of what might happen next.

He was exhausted and began to feel as though he would be overcome with vertigo. Certain he had angered whatever was in the opening, he closed his eyes. If his head cleared of the dizziness, he hoped he would be better prepared to deal with whatever came next.

Bob was unaware he had dropped to his knees. He wasn't sure if what he began to experience was real or imagined. He flinched suddenly because he felt a burning sensation.

Nearly molten sand shot violently into his face and on his torso, as the opening began to reestablish its presence. He screamed from the pain, but no one heard him. Through the blast of sand that punished him with burns to his exposed skin, he again saw the red dots. They weren't dots any longer. They were larger now and beet red with anger.

The red dots. Are they Shadow's eyes? Damn! This can't be happening! This can't be happening, he thought.

In the midst of the cloud of sand that filled the space between Bob and the opening, he saw him. It was a young boy. No more than twelve or thirteen. His body didn't stand out from the sand cloud, it was part of it. The boy appeared to be trying to run from the opening, but he was being forcefully drawn back into it, his body stretching rearward. He was being sucked into the opening.

And then, it was quiet. When he dared open his eyes, Bob saw that the opening remained covered with sand. He stood, not bothering to brush the sand from the knees of his jeans. There had been no attack from the hole...at least not yet. He squinted again and tried to control his breathing. He wasn't convinced the danger of violent eruption had passed.

Oh, God, he thought. *What just happened?*

13

"You do know you're breaking the law, right?"

The voice was unexpected, but it was familiar. It came from the condo's boardwalk. Bob turned slowly.

"Is that you, Malia Matthews? You have certainly caught me in a very compromising position," Bob said. He began to walk toward her. He felt a certain degree of confidence turning his back on the now buried hole. He couldn't say why, but he didn't think there would be a reaction from the opening in the presence of witnesses.

"Careful, now. You don't want to screw up the dune while you're on one of your nature walks, do you?" She was barely able to control her laughter.

"I guess I deserve to hear my own words played back to me," Bob said. He decided to tell her the truth, but not the whole truth. "Actually, every so often, some of us in the community walk carefully through the dune to retrieve the trash people deposit in here accidentally or intentionally."

"You aren't carrying any trash, Commodore," she said.

"What? Yes, well, I just got started and something distracted me."

Bob made gradual progress toward the edge of the dune, but, each time he spoke to her, he stopped and leaned gently on his walking stick. Malia's tongue-in-cheek guidance aside, he needed his undivided attention to be on where he stepped. He practiced what he preached about not harming the dune, but, truth be told, his legs were a little rubbery after what he had just experienced. He wasn't sure how much of his performance Malia had witnessed.

"Oh, Jesus. I don't like the looks of this, Mary," Tony said to his wife as he looked out through the sliding glass door in his living room.

"What's the matter?" she asked.

"This is what I was talking about. Look. Bob is standing in the dune and it looks as though he's having a conversation."

"So? Maybe he is," she said.

"So, nothing. He's there by himself. There is nobody else there with him. What the hell is he doing in the dune anyway? He actually told me he met a young girl the other day and that she appeared out of nowhere from the dune."

"Are you kidding?" she asked.

"I'm dead serious. It sounded to me like he imagined the whole thing. I bet he thinks he's talking to her now. I need to check on line to see if hallucinations are a symptom of dementia. Wasn't there something on TV last week about Parkinson's disease and hallucinations? I know I heard something about that the other day."

"Oh, honey, this is so sad," Mary said. "We may have to do something to get him help."

Tony was concerned about his friend's welfare. From the start, he was skeptical of Bob's story about Malia and his sudden infatuation with the mysteries of the dune. It never occurred to Tony to step out onto his balcony for a better look at Bob. Had he done so, he would have seen Malia and a young man standing on the boardwalk.

"Malia, are you going to introduce me to this young man?" Bob said as he stepped up out of the dune.

"I am. Commodore Bob, this is Devlin Pryor, my friend from school. Devlin, meet Commodore Bob."

"Sir, it's a pleasure to meet you. Malia didn't realize how much of a legend you are in Virginia Beach," Devlin said.

"A legend? Is that what people say I am?" Bob asked.

"Yeah, Devlin's been telling me a lot of stories about you, Commodore. He told me you are a war hero and that you were in charge of one of the Navy bases before you left the Navy. Let's see, what else? He told me about your work to start the Norfolk Aquarium and to clean up the Chesapeake Bay. Word is, the Bay wouldn't be safe to swim in if it wasn't for you."

"Well, Malia, Devlin is very kind, but overly generous in his praise. I am certainly not a war hero. I served my country proudly in times of war and peace, but a hero I am not. I may have accomplished a few things in my life, but nobody gets anything done without the help of many others," Bob said. "I've received more credit than I deserve for a lot of things."

"Malia, don't forget about the boys in the ocean," Devlin said.

"Oh, yeah," she added. "In the library, we pulled up *The Virginian-Pilot* story about the two boys you saved from drowning in the ocean years ago."

"Rescuing one person is heroic, Commodore," Devlin said. "But swimming out again, in time to save another boy is awesome."

"You have to read the whole story, kids," Bob said, leaning again on the walking stick. "I didn't get back out there in time to save their brother. That's the part I remember most about that day."

"What you did was still brave, Commodore," Devlin said.

"It sure was. Wasn't it at night, after the lifeguards were off duty?"

"Yes. Technically, the beach was closed to swimmers. The boys were out on a raft. Way too dangerous. I'll tell you, though, I find it curious that story is still being told and that people of your generation have any idea who I am. But that's enough about me," Bob said.

"Well, I've told Devlin all about the dune and the stories you've told me," Malia said.

"She really has, sir. I never heard all that stuff about Marco Polo and I am dying to know more about the dune. It all sounds so cool."

"And a little bit scary," Malia added.

"No way," Devlin countered. "I'm not worried about that. I want to know as much as I can about the dune. I want to explore it."

"Careful, Devlin. My mother always says that curiosity killed the cat," Malia said.

Bob's mind projected the image of Shadow, Joan Mulligan's dead cat, encountered only minutes before.

"That's okay, Malia. I really don't like cats," Devlin said, with a laugh.

Humor, Bob thought. *If you can't admit you're afraid of something, why not laugh at it?*

"Your mother is right, Malia," Bob finally spoke. "Look, kids, I'm about to go upstairs, but…"

"Oh, no, Commodore Bob. You promised the next time I came by, we would sit at one of the picnic tables by the crossover."

"We will, Malia. I just want to put on a dry shirt and get a cold drink. Can I get you both something?"

"No, we're good. We both have water bottles," Malia said. "But, please bring Pepper back with you."

"You'll just spoil him worse than he already is, but I'll bring him down. See you in a few minutes."

"You must have seen a lot of action with that walking stick, Commodore," Devlin said. "The end of it looks like it's been in a fire."

"Oh, I've seen my share," Bob said, as he raised the stick a few inches off the ground and looked at its end. He realized his response seemed almost flippant. He didn't want to be dismissive of the kid, but Devlin's observation caught Bob off guard. "I'll be down in just a minute."

He began to walk up the outside back staircase. When he got to the second landing, he saw that Malia and Devlin had their backs to him. He stopped to examine the walking stick closely. The end was clearly charred. Bob knew it must have happened when he probed the opening.

There was no open fire on the beach, you dummy, he thought. *What you smelled was your own walking stick starting to burn.*

Bob felt a chill that comes when you realize you may have just escaped a very dangerous situation.

"I guess that's better than smelling my own flesh burn," he said quietly, as he resumed his walk up the stairs. A feeling of nausea rose within him as he grasped the reality of how close he may have come to a violent encounter with the opening.

14

Malia and Devlin walked slowly to the table where Bob promised to join them. Devlin stopped about halfway there.

"What do you think, Malia? Do you think the dune is really haunted?"

"Nobody ever said it was haunted," Malia responded.

"The Commodore just about did."

"He said it was dangerous. And, yes, I think he meant it. Anyway, why would Commodore Bob lie to me?"

"It isn't like the old guy is lying. It could be he only wants to protect the dune. You just about said so yourself. So, he decides to tell some scary stories to get your attention and keep you from going into the dune."

"I suppose. But he's a nice old man and I think he enjoys the company. I told my mom and dad about Bob and how I'm kind of doing a good deed by spending time with him. My mom thinks it's nice, but my dad told me I'm not allowed to go to his apartment. As though I would. He also said I have to tell him if Bob ever invites me in. Crazy, huh? I can't imagine Bob attacking me. Can you?"

"I doubt it. I definitely don't get that vibe from him at all, but it would be cool to see the inside of his condo. I bet it's filled with things from when he was in the Navy. Did he tell you if he was ever assigned in the South Pacific? I wonder if he has any shrunken heads on a bookshelf or something."

"Devlin, you really do have a weird side, don't you?"

"Okay. Maybe there is some kind of danger in the dune,

but look at it. It's a dune, for God's sake. The grass is taller than us, but it isn't a forest. It doesn't have quicksand or anything like that."

"What's your point?" she asked.

"I'm just saying. If I go into the dune, right?"

"Wrong."

"I'm just saying. Say I go into the dune—into the very middle of it—and say I see something dangerous. All I would have to do is run either toward the water or toward Bob's condo building. It's three stories high. I'd be able to see it from anywhere in there. It just isn't that far to go to get out of trouble."

"I hear what you're saying. In a way, you're right."

"See."

"No. I'm only saying when Bob saw me walking in the dune, I never felt like I was in any danger. I wasn't there to do damage to the dune. I was just walking on the beach, thinking about my finals. I can't tell you why I walked into the dune. I just felt like it for some reason."

"Bob might tell you something lured you in there and that he saved you from something before it had the opportunity to hurt you. I'm saying I doubt if that's really it. I think you and I ought to go into the dune just to prove it isn't this mysterious place. Do you want to try it?"

"Now? No way," Malia said. "Bob would be angry and disappointed if he came down here and you and I were in the dune. It would break his heart."

"All right. Okay. But I'm not saying I'm never going to do it. Just not right now," Devlin said.

Malia's face lit up with a broad smile. She got up from the bench. "Here comes that adorable dog. Hello, Pepper!"

Bob had Pepper on the leash, but he dropped it on the boardwalk when Malia moved toward them. Pepper ran to her. She facilitated the dog's show of affection by sitting on the boardwalk. Bob walked passed them and joined Devlin at the table.

"He'll lick you until his tongue falls off, if you let him," Bob said.

Malia stood with Pepper in her arms. The love-fest continued as she walked toward the table.

"You're just the sweetest dog in the world. I think I'll take you home, you gorgeous animal."

"And people think I'm delusional," Bob said to Devlin, motioning with his head to Malia.

Bob unscrewed the lid of his bottle of iced tea and took a sip.

"I'm sorry it took me so long to come back down," Bob said. "I called one of my neighbors, but she and her husband aren't home. So, I left a message."

"That's okay, sir," Devlin said.

So, Devlin, what makes you so curious about the dune?"

"Well, sir, my grandfather used to tell me ghost stories about Virginia Beach, the Chesapeake Bay, and the ocean."

"Was your grandfather in the Navy?"

"Merchant Marine, sir," Devlin answered. "His stories got me into reading a lot of sci-fi and even some horror novels. My mother used to tell him to stop, but that only made me more interested. When Malia told me about her visits with you, I told her I would really like to meet you."

"Devlin, the stories I've shared with Malia aren't science fiction. And while some of them might make the hairs on the back of your neck stand up, I wouldn't call them horror stories, either. But that's really beside the point because…"

"But some can be pretty scary," Devlin cut him off.

"Sure, but what I was going to say is that the stories I've

shared with Malia have more than a grain of truth to them. Over time, people may have enhanced the reality. That's how I'd like to say it because there truly is a reality part to each story."

"My grandfather used to say the same thing about his stories. If he thought they were completely made up, he would say so, but I'm sure he thought most of the stories he told me were pretty much true."

They talked more about the dune and Marco Polo. Bob repeated a couple of the stories he had already told Malia.

"I don't want to repeat myself too much and I know Malia has told you this," Bob said. "But preserving this dune is very important to me."

"Yes, sir," Devlin said.

At this point, Malia had become more spectator than participant. She split her attention between Devlin's conversation with Bob and Pepper's incessant need for attention.

"But I have to tell you kids—and please share this with your friends—over the last week, I've had a real sense that something bad is going on in the dune. I don't want to sound melodramatic, but I'm worried that the dune, or something in it, is extremely dangerous. I don't know if it's a prowler, an animal, or something else, but I don't think it's anything to be taken lightly."

"Oh, God, Commodore. Have you told the police?" Malia was now reengaged in the conversation.

"They'll tell me no crime has been committed. And they'd be right. Even Animal Control would balk at chasing a shadow or an old man's intuition. No. I'll just have to wait and watch, but, in the meantime, it has me worried."

"If it isn't a prowler or an animal, what else could it be?" Malia asked.

There was a marked difference between Malia's facial expression and that of Devlin. Malia wore a look of concern for Bob, who was clearly struggling internally. Devlin, on the other hand, was wide-eyed. His interest peaked. The vagueness of Bob's words only excited Devlin's curiosity.

"That's a good question," Bob replied.

"Oh, man," Devlin said. "This is sooo cool!"

"Commodore Bob, I'm sure there's some kind of animal hanging out in the dune, and before you know it, you'll see it. Then, the mystery will be gone and you won't have to worry about it so much. When you saw me in the dune, there was nothing else there. I didn't see anything."

Bob knew Malia was trying to put him at ease. He'd only known her for a few days. Yet, his expression of concern must have been so obvious even this young girl could see it.

I'm happy I didn't tell them about my encounter with the opening. If I did, I think Malia would have developed an ulcer on my behalf and Devlin would lose control of his bladder out of excitement, he thought.

"Thank you, Malia. I appreciate that," Bob said.

"Wait a minute, Commodore. If you're so sure the dune is dangerous, why were you in there alone when we got here?" Devlin asked. The look on his face begged Bob to let him in on the excitement.

"Devlin!" Malia said sharply. "You shouldn't ask The Commodore that." But she was wondering the same thing.

"No, Malia, Devlin has a point. Good for you to pick up on that, Devlin."

"You weren't in there looking for trash, were you?" he said.

"Well, while it's true that some of us go into the dune periodically for that reason, that isn't what I was doing."

"I knew it!" Devlin was almost gleeful.

"Truth is, I thought I saw something in the dune and I went in to investigate."

"Commodore, you shouldn't be going into the dune alone. Not after what you just told us," Malia said.

"You're probably right, Malia. And I can tell you one thing. I won't be going in there again anytime soon. Not until the little voice in my head stops sending me warning signals."

"We can go back in together, if you want, Commodore. I'll go in with you."

"No, Devlin. Thanks for the offer, but I've had enough adventure for one day. Maybe another time."

"Any time, sir. You just say the word."

The three of them took a drink from their respective bottles. Malia turned her attention back to Pepper.

"Well, what else do you kids have planned for today? Hanging out with an old fart like me can't be the highlight of your day."

"Oh, Commodore Bob, you know you're always the highlight of my day," Malia said with a smile. "Devlin and I are going to walk over to the donut shop on Shore Drive to celebrate the end of exams. Well, Devlin's exams, to be exact. I have one more tomorrow," Malia said.

"Yeah, I had my last two today," Devlin added.

"I have my mom's car. So, I'll drive Devlin to his house. He's only about a mile away."

"If that," Devlin said. "I'm right off North Great Neck, just after the small bridge over the channel."

"That's a bit more than a mile," Bob added.

"And then I'll go home for dinner. It's my brother's birthday. He gets to pick what we have for dinner. Then, I'll study," Malia said.

"Whoa, donuts and birthday cake on the same day," Bob said.

"Yeah, I know," Malia said.

"How about you, Devlin?" Bob asked.

"I'm home for dinner, too. I guess I'll watch a movie or play a video game or something. My way of partying by myself, I guess. Tomorrow, I'm going to Jennie Adams' end-of-year party. Are you going, Malia?"

"Yep. Sure am."

"Hey, Commodore," Devlin said. "Before we go, I wanted to ask if you ever heard reports about the Navy SEALs using this beach for war games. Maybe it's the SEALs doing things in the dune."

"Oh, God. Not that again," Bob reacted. "Devlin, I'm not going to ask you where you heard that nonsense. I don't want to know, but trust me when I tell you it isn't true. The SEALs do not conduct military maneuvers on this beach. Never did. If I live to be two hundred years old, I hope I never hear that nonsense again."

"Sorry, sir. I didn't mean to make you angry."

"Oh, I'm not angry, son. Not at all. It just amazes me that the most ridiculous stories are the ones that seem to have the longest lives."

Malia and Devlin stood to leave. They said their goodbyes to Bob and Pepper.

"I enjoyed our conversation. Be careful and, remember, be nice to the dune," Bob said. "Have a great summer."

"You can't get rid of me that easy, Commodore Bob," Malia said. "I'll see you again soon."

"I'll be here." Bob picked up Pepper's leash. "Along with my furry friend."

Rather than walk on the beach to the public access path, Bob invited them to go with him through the pool area and the condo parking lot to get to the street. Bob carried Pepper (as the condo rules required) across the pool deck and then let him walk on the leash through the parking lot. When they reached Page Avenue, Bob went left with the dog toward the curbside mailboxes that serviced the Bay Ridge Condominiums. Malia and Devlin walked in the opposite direction toward the donut shop.

The content of Bob's mailbox was unremarkable today. Bob and Pepper headed back to the condo parking lot. This was his first opportunity to think about the harrowing experience he had in the dune just before Malia and Devlin arrived.

Bob knew it would take him some time to process all that happened in that brief period of time. What was real? What was imagined? An unsettled feeling came to his stomach again.

Pepper was content to sniff everything he could within the length of his leash. Bob didn't rush the dog. He was lost in his thoughts and, without really thinking about it, walked with Pepper much farther than he had intended. At one point, he stood still on the sidewalk, allowing the dog to sniff extensively again. Finally, a car horn snapped him out of it. He looked up quickly enough to see Malia drive by. She and Devlin waved.

"Let's go home, Pepper. I need a shower and we need to think about dinner," Bob said to the dog.

15

When they entered his unit, Bob proceeded directly to the kitchen. It had been a very long day and Bob had a lot to process. He was grateful for the visit by Malia and Devlin, but he was tired. Even though he'd had a decent amount of sleep, it came after he woke up in his living room at 2:00 a.m. with the TV on.

When he was standing in the dune, facing the opening that had been obscured by sand, he could not imagine a favorable outcome. The sound of Malia's voice was like a light going on in a dark room. His sense of gloom vanished instantly. He found it odd that her sudden presence could have this effect.

There's something special about that kid, he thought.

He also wondered what would be next for him and for the dune. Bob knew shoving sand into the opening was not going to be enough to end the threat or get it to retreat to wherever it goes when it isn't here. If anything, he was sure he had only pissed it off. It troubled him and even made him a bit scared.

Bob washed his hands at the kitchen sink. He put the remaining leftover pasta on a plate and started the microwave.

"Pepper, I believe I'm going to turn into a plate of spaghetti. This is the last of it, kiddo. No more carbs for the rest of the month, after this. Now let's go out and take a quick look at the dune."

Bob moved through the living room to the sliding glass door. Rather than follow him, Pepper jumped onto the couch and curled up on an end cushion.

"Done for the day?" Bob asked, noticing he had been abandoned by the dog.

Two steps onto the balcony and Bob broke stride awkwardly. He came close to falling as he avoided whatever it was he nearly stepped on. It was the kind of maneuver people Bob's age shouldn't be able to do. Those who try often break a hip after they fall.

Bob had certainly put on a few pounds since his days in uniform, but he retained an athlete's agility. He grabbed the railing with both hands, stabilized himself, and stared at the bowel movement Pepper had deposited on the balcony.

"Pepper, when the hell did you do this?" Bob couldn't believe he hadn't seen it when he came upstairs earlier to change his shirt, get a drink, and place a call to the Mulligans about their cat, Shadow. Of course, at the time, he was more attentive to his charred walking stick, his promise to get back downstairs, and more than a little shaken by his encounter in the dune.

The treat Bob had given the dog before he had gone into the dune was on the floor, only half-eaten. That was enough evidence for Bob to conclude that the dog had been acutely aware of the danger Bob faced in the dune.

"I guess I wasn't the only one who had the crap scared out of him when I was down there," he said, as he cleaned up after Pepper and flushed the load down the toilet.

Bob ignored the periodic beeping that signaled the microwave had reheated his food. He stepped outside again to take advantage of the time before dusk to survey the dune and the Bay. The sliding door was slightly ajar. He could see that the coaler was not present, and with the help of his binoculars, he was surprised to see that the opening appeared to still be covered over with sand. This made no sense to him.

Bob had assumed his actions in the dune earlier in the day would have angered whatever was there. He expected immediate retribution, but there was none. He concluded the presence of Malia and Devlin helped put off the inevitable. But, he certainly expected the opening to have reappeared by now.

"Well, maybe I was wrong," Bob said. "I'm glad Tony isn't around to hear me say that."

Bob's attention was drawn from the dune when he heard the rattle of Pepper's license and ID tags as the dog shook. Until then, Bob hadn't noticed that Pepper had joined him on the balcony. The microwave beeped again and Bob turned to retrieve his dinner.

"I refuse to believe all this went away because I stood up to the bully and kicked sand in his face," he said aloud to himself. "That would be too good to be true."

The food was still hot enough for Bob. He sat down to eat his dinner with the local and national news on the television in the background. "No ballgame tonight, Pepper. It's you, me, Lester Holt, Alex Trebek, the crossword puzzle, and goodnight, sweet prince."

Bob easily stayed awake through *Jeopardy*, but he fell asleep not long thereafter, with the crossword puzzle in his lap.

At around 10:30, Bob woke, changed into his pajamas (a pair of shorts and an oversized black tee shirt), brushed his teeth, and pulled down the bedspread. Pepper didn't need an invitation. He was lying by one of Bob's pillows as soon as he heard the sound of the bed being undone.

"Not so fast, kiddo. Come on, we'll break the rules one more time."

Pepper followed Bob onto the balcony and moved quickly through the door and down the back stairs. As he usually did when he utilized this unorthodox method of walking his dog, Bob looked down onto the boardwalk, ready to order the dog home if he wandered out too far.

The dog never appeared on the boardwalk. Bob leaned out as far as he could, but still, no evidence of Pepper. He felt his anxiety level rise.

No, please. Don't make this the way you get payback for sparing me this afternoon. Don't go after my dog. Bob made his plea silently to the dune. He had the awful image in his mind of Pepper lying in the dune, his body flattened like the body of Joan Mulligan's cat.

Bob felt a distinct level of discomfort in his stomach. For all his talk, Bob loved that little dog and now he was convinced he had sent the poor thing to its demise.

Unconcerned that he was wearing pajamas and slippers, Bob moved to the stairway door resolved to confront the sad reality. And then he heard it. It was faint at first, but then a little louder. It was a scratch at the door, followed by a whimper.

With his hand on the doorknob, he stopped to consider that this could be a trap. Was Pepper injured? Was Pepper dead and was something else on the other side of the door waiting for him?

Bob listened. Something was definitely breathing on the third floor landing. He thought about saying the dog's name, but wasn't convinced that would be a smart thing to do. He crossed over to the other end of the balcony and retrieved his walking stick from the shed. Back to the stairway door, Bob took a deep breath and readied himself for an assault from the unknown.

"Please, God. Spare that little dog."

He turned the knob and pulled open the door.

"Oh, for God's sake. I'm such an idiot."

Pepper, tail wagging, walked quickly onto the balcony

and to the glass slider. Bob secured the stairway door, leaned the walking stick against one of the tall chairs, and followed the dog into the condo.

By then, it was too dark for Bob to have seen that the opening had again formed in the same location. And, with all the activity surrounding Pepper and the stairway, Bob never looked out into the Bay, where he would have been able to see the broken pattern of the lights on the Bridge-Tunnel caused by the return of the coaler.

"Here I was, prepared to die for you and all the while you were down and back and waiting to come inside. I'm going to have to teach you to pee in the toilet."

The 11:00 news was broadcasting on the bedroom television. Bob forgot to set the sleep timer, but the TV would not keep him awake tonight. Before the weatherman was predicting the likelihood of thunderstorms by the Bay through the night, Bob and Pepper were asleep.

16

Devlin started the evening at home. The seniors agreed the partying would wait for Friday and Saturday, when every member of the class would be finished with high school exams forever.

With his parents upstairs in the living room, Devlin planted himself on the basement couch to watch a movie or two and play video games.

"It's nearly 11:00, Devlin. Mom and I are going to bed," his father said.

"Not everybody is lucky enough to have tomorrow off," his mother chimed in, with a smile in her voice.

"It isn't luck, mom. It's scheduling skill," Devlin said, continuing the joke.

"Okay, Mr. Schedule Genius," his mother said, "don't stay up too late and be sure to turn off the lights when you go up to bed."

"Got it, Mom. Goodnight."

All evening, regardless of what he was watching or what game he was playing, his mind repeatedly returned to the visit with The Commodore. More than that, though, he was obsessed with the dune.

During the ride home with Malia, Devlin tried to convince her that Bob had overstated the situation as a way to protect the dune and to keep kids out. He was sure of it. He also told her that he suspected The Commodore might be hiding something in the dune he didn't want them to find. Malia dismissed that theory, but she was unable to change Devlin's mind. He was resolved to go into the dune with or without her. He just didn't know when.

Sitting on the couch in his parent's basement, Devlin swallowed a sizable swig of a high-caffeine energy drink and said aloud in a voice intended only for his own ears, "Now is about as good a time as any, I suppose."

At that point, Devlin methodically went through the house, preparing for his departure. He left a video game on the television and lowered the volume. He turned off the lights, as his mother had asked. Then, he quietly climbed the stairs to the second floor, pulled down his bedspread, and rustled the sheets.

Devlin used the old trick of laying pillows end-to-end, mimicking his body in the bed. If his parents looked in on him before he returned, they would surely think he was in bed. If, instead, one of them wandered downstairs and looked briefly into the basement, the light from the television would make them think he was still down there either playing a video game or stretched out on the couch. Devlin had done this more than once on weekends and his parents always left him undisturbed. Besides, he would be back in a couple of hours—three at the most, long before they got up for work.

Devlin switched from shorts to jeans. He might not know everything that was in the dune, but he was sure there would be bugs. He took a roll of quarters from his dresser drawer, and on his way back into the basement, he grabbed his hooded windbreaker from the hall closet. He ensured the first floor doors—front, rear, and garage access—were locked with their deadbolts.

He used the light from the television to transit to the basement door that led to the backyard. Even if he returned later than expected, he knew he could enter the house unnoticed and, if necessary, pretend he had fallen asleep in the basement while playing one last video game.

It was 1:30 in the morning when he put on his Norfolk Tides baseball cap, walked out and began the trek to the beach. With his hands buried in his windbreaker pockets, he walked quickly along the wide sidewalk of North Great Neck Road. The air was damp. It felt as though it might rain.

He told himself he had to look like an adult walking with a destination in mind.

Slow down. You don't want a cop to think you're leaving the scene of a crime, he thought.

Most importantly, he did not want to look like a kid who snuck out of the house in the middle of the night.

At the intersection of North Great Neck Road and Shore Drive, he turned west. He began to perspire, but his breathing was only slightly heavier than when he started out. He saw the sky brighten suddenly with the lightning of an approaching storm. Seconds thereafter, he heard the rolling thunder. The storm sounded far away. He hadn't thought to check the weather forecast, but it wouldn't have mattered. Tonight was his night to explore the dune. Tomorrow, he would tell Malia all about it.

Have to be sure to take a selfie or two for Malia, he told himself.

Devlin was surprised there was so much traffic on Shore Drive at this hour. He thought the passing traffic would make his journey less threatening. Nonetheless, his right hand was wrapped tightly around the $10 roll of quarters. Just in case he had to defend himself against a mugger, the quarters would enhance the force of his fist. At least, he hoped it would. He remembered seeing this done in a movie.

Devlin could see the realtor's office ahead on the corner. He knew he was getting closer to his destination. His pace quickened. A right turn, followed by a quick left and he would be on Page Avenue, approaching the Bay Ridge

Condominium complex. Rather than risk confronting someone from the condos, Devlin decided to walk past the property, to the beach's public access path.

When his feet touched the sand on the access path, Devlin felt his heartbeat increase. He was excited. Not even the lightning that was getting closer or the thunder that followed could dampen his mood now.

Here he was. On the beach. Standing directly across from The Commodore's balcony. Or, as the old man would call it, his lanai. There was a dim, flickering light behind the curtains in one of the rooms. Devlin correctly guessed it was Bob's television, playing for a sleeping dog and his master.

"Here goes nothing," Devlin said, as he stepped forward into the dune. Almost as though he had tripped an invisible switch, a steady rain began to fall with his first step. Devlin continued moving forward.

"Slowly but surely," he said softly.

The loss of moonlight and the growing intensity of the rainfall made it difficult for Devlin to see more than a few feet in front of him. Were it not for the lights on the landings of the condo's back staircase, he would have been functionally blind.

The exceptions to this were those brief moments when the dune appeared to be bathed in daylight thanks to a bolt of lightning centered somewhere overhead. But that light was brief, sudden, and unpredictable. Devlin was not able to take advantage of it. And when the lightning came, Devlin swore he could feel it as much as see it. The thunder that now followed was nearly immediate and it shook the ground.

"Well, this may not have been the brightest idea I've ever had," he said aloud to himself. His saturated jeans felt at least twice their normal weight and his windbreaker was clearly not as water resistant as advertised. The rain had soaked through to his skin.

He looked right and left as he advanced into the dune. His hope of finding something awesome in the dune was replaced with the more immediate goal of getting to the boardwalk and using it, the pool deck, and the parking lot to start his journey home. At this point, he didn't care who he might meet in the parking lot.

Devlin moved his hands quickly to keep his hood from slipping from his head. As he did, he half-turned to his right. At that moment, and only for a moment, the dune was alive with bright light that rivaled noon on a brilliantly sunny day. He heard the sizzle of the lightning and felt the concussion of the thunder throughout his body.

That's when he saw it.

Even though I walk through the valley of the shadow of death, I will fear no evil, for you are at my side. Your rod and your staff give me courage.

Psalm 23

Friday

17

"Shit," Devlin said, as an uncontrolled reaction to what he had seen in the seconds-long, lightning-produced daylight. But what had he seen? It was something like a large black circle. It was probably on the sand, but Devlin could swear it was floating just off the dune surface. The white light had nearly disabled his sense of depth and proportion.

Maybe it wasn't a circle at all. It could have been an object. Maybe it was a box or a chest of some kind. As his mind raced, it sped to conclusions with no basis in fact. In his mind, he saw a treasure chest. He imagined the riches it might hold.

Maybe this is why the old guy doesn't want anyone in the dune. He's got a stash of valuables here. Booty from his days at sea, Devlin thought.

Almost immediately, another thought occurred to him, but this time he said it aloud in a low voice.

"If Malia was here, she would tell me what a dumb idea that was."

Devlin reached into his jacket pocket with his left hand. He pulled out his phone and activated its flashlight function. He was essentially shining light on a thick wall of rain. The light beam couldn't reach the surface of the dune.

Realizing it was useless, he slid his right index finger across the screen in an effort to turn off the flashlight. The phone slipped from his wet hands. Instinctively, he reached down, attempting to catch the phone before it hit the ground. When his left hand touched the phone in mid-air, he wasn't able to grip it. Instead, he slapped it somewhere to his right in the direction of the object he had seen in that brief moment of lightning.

"Damn!" he said.

The phone landed, face down. Devlin spotted the dim beam of the flashlight shining up into the rain. He moved a few steps toward it.

Lightning again. Thunder. At least as intense as before.

Devlin saw the dark circle again, but the light didn't last long enough for him to focus on it. He bent slowly and picked up his phone. He tried one more time to shine the light in the direction of the object which was now slightly more than his body length away. The flashlight was still no help. He clutched the phone tightly this time and successfully turned off the light.

He put the phone in his jacket and zipped the pocket closed in a useless effort to keep the phone dry.

And then it touched him.

It was as though a fan was blowing warm air at him from the same direction as the black circle. He turned to face it. Despite the rain, Devlin was able to distinguish the outside edge of the warm air stream coming at him and the distinct temperature difference inside and outside the column of forced air.

He squinted, but could see nothing of the black circle, which he now assumed was some kind of vent emitting air that was getting warmer. He stepped closer. Warmer still. Another step. The column of air felt hot now.

It irritated his exposed face, but, at the same time, soothed his body that had been chilled by the rain and his saturated clothes. Devlin held his hands out in front of his face to shield it while he peered through parted fingers.

Another step. And then, another.

Lightning again. Thunder.

He saw it more clearly this time. He was close enough. The black circle had dimension. It was an opening of some kind in the dune's surface. Devlin leaned forward, now hoping for another burst of lightning to enable him to see it better.

"Come on," he said. "One more time. I bet I'm looking right at it. Come on!"

As if on command, the sky exploded with sudden light. He was looking directly at the opening and what he saw turned his curiosity into horror. He wanted to run, but his legs would not move. He was frozen in place. He prayed there would be no more lightning. He had seen enough.

Indeed, there would be no additional lightning—at least not in the dune. The sky above the Bay lit briefly with reflected brightness from lightning that had moved on. To confirm its distance, the thunder took longer to announce itself and it did so with a rolling rumble somewhere over the clouds. The rain stopped. The passing storm had cooled the night air.

Almost immediately, the slight evening breeze made Devlin feel cold. As he dug into his jacket's left pocket for his phone, he shifted his position left and right until he again felt the hot air coming from the opening. It was better than being cold. The rain saturated and dissolved the paper wrapped around the quarters in his right jacket pocket. Every move he made was now accompanied by the sound of forty loose quarters shifting in the zippered pocket.

Devlin had trouble manipulating the touch screen on his phone. At first, he thought his hands were cramping and figured it was due to the rain and the change in air temperature.

"What the hell is going on?" he said softly, beginning to show frustration with his sudden lack of dexterity.

His hands weren't cramping. That wasn't it. He soon realized that swiping his phone's screen required him to resist some kind of a force that was pulling at his hands. He could now feel it tugging at his chest, trying to draw him forward. Devlin finally managed to activate the phone's camera, but, as he turned it toward the opening, it again slipped (or was pulled) from his hand.

To make matters worse, it began to rain again. No lightning. No thunder. Just a heavy rain pouring straight down from the clouds.

Leaning forward to pick up the phone proved not to be his smartest move. Clutching the phone tightly, Devlin struggled to straighten. The air was hotter and it appeared to have shifted its aim so that it continued to blow directly on him, even though his profile was lower than before. He was confused by his lack of control. The hot air was blowing in a strong column directly in his face, but he was being simultaneously pulled forward.

His disorientation was fed by sudden vertigo. He wasn't sure if what he saw was real or imagined. Everything seemed to speed up in a now dizzying environment. He thought he saw a black cat with flame-red eyes. There was a barefoot kid in loose-fitting clothes, his age or a little younger, straining to get away from something invisible that seemed to pull him backward by his shoulders. A group of a dozen or so stood off to the side. Men and women in their twenties, standing together wearing bathing suits. And, now, sailors (or were they pirates?) leaning on the railing of a ship. No, wait. Maybe they were on The Commodore's damn lanai. And wasn't that The Commodore standing there with them?

Only The Commodore appeared to have a normal body. The others now appeared more like hand puppets when contrasted with The Commodore's body. Their eyes were red. Everyone had red eyes that stared at him. Everyone except The Commodore.

They mocked him.

The Commodore's face showed signs of worry and

concern. He was definitely speaking to Devlin, but there was no way Devlin could hear what he was saying. He seemed to be reaching out to Devlin, stretching his arms over the balcony railing, but the distance between them was far too great for any physical contact.

Devlin felt pain. It was a pain that filled his body. Because of his disorientation, he was unaware that, though his feet were firmly planted in the dune, his body was nearly parallel to the ground. Additionally, it had been grotesquely stretched to an inhuman appearance.

It took all the strength he could muster to lift his head, but Devlin wanted to see whatever was drawing him forward. He was more scared than he had ever been in his young life. He wanted to cry, but he was also angry and, right now, anger ruled.

When he was finally able to look into the opening, his vision was distorted, as though he was looking through a fish-eye lens. The hot air burned his face. The pull was so intense, he could not form words. He saw only two small red lights.

As if his body were not grotesque enough, Devlin's mouth was drawn open. A viscous substance began to flow from within him, into the opening. And, then, it was quiet.

Devlin was gone. A bright light appeared briefly on the bridge of the coaler, at anchor near the Bridge-Tunnel, but it was obscured by the heavy rain.

18

The light that made its way through the drawn, nearly sheer curtains told Bob that it was morning. He did not feel rested and he ached. His back, his neck, and his arms all hurt from the exertion he put himself through the previous day.

Old men should not be stalking around in the dune, challenging unseen enemies or climbing multiple flights of stairs in the same day, he told himself.

Bob couldn't recall if (or how many times) his sleep had been disturbed overnight. He remembered intense thunder and lightning. He guessed it went on for almost fifteen minutes, but he had no idea what time that was. Bob was right about the storm's intensity, but he underestimated its length by half. When the lightning finally stopped, the rumble of thunder in the distance continued for another thirty minutes or so.

And then it was gone. The sky began to clear and, before dawn, stars could be seen in the sky over the Bay.

Except for the interruptions that brought him to semi-consciousness (and two trips to the bathroom), Bob had been asleep. It was also unlikely anyone noticed that the coaler, at anchor by the bridge expanse, seemed to come alive briefly with lights that flickered on the ship's deck. Bob saw none of this, of course.

He threw his legs over the side of his bed and his feet found his slippers. He reached for the remote. It had been a while since he had gone to bed without using the TV's sleep timer. He wasn't happy with himself for forgetting to set it.

As he yawned and tried wiping the sleep from his eyes, Bob realized, even with the television turned off, he continued to hear an undercurrent of noise. It was definitely the sound of conversations. Three, maybe four voices going back and forth.

Because his front door was so close to the elevator, it was not unusual for owners, visitors, delivery personnel, or repairmen to linger there. Fighting his sore muscles, Bob walked slowly out of his bedroom and looked to his left, down the hall. With the front door in sight, Bob would be able to see the silhouette of anyone standing outside through the door's smoked glass panel. No one was there, but, from where he now stood, he could tell the voices were coming from the Bay side of the condo.

He could see that no one was on his balcony. Based on the volume, Bob concluded the voices were coming from the boardwalk area. They were too distinct to be on the beach.

As much as he wanted a cup of coffee and a couple of Aleve to go with his morning vitamin and blood pressure medication, curiosity won out. Bob moved to the back door and stepped onto the balcony. Pepper joined him, tail wagging, expecting his daily trip down the back stairs was mere seconds away.

Immediately as he stepped onto the balcony, Bob's face filled with an anger strong enough to allow him to forget about his muscle ache.

"What the hell do you think you're doing?"

The man in the black VABPD windbreaker turned and looked up at Bob from the dune. The half dozen others (five uniform police and a woman also wearing a VABPD windbreaker) stopped briefly, but then went back to their work, clearly searching the dune for something.

"Go back inside, sir. We'll be up to see you very soon. We're conducting an investigation here," the man in the windbreaker said.

"The hell you are," Bob responded, no less angry. "You're screwing up the dune is what you're doing. What the hell are you looking for?"

"Sir, do you see that yellow tape?" the windbreaker pointed toward the area where Bob had encountered the opening yesterday. A rectangular portion of the dune was cordoned off with yellow tape. Bob had not noticed it until now.

"That's called crime scene tape and it would not be unreasonable for you to assume this, sir, is a crime scene. Now, give me your apartment number and I'll be up in a minute to see you."

"I'm pretty familiar with the dune, officer. I was in there as recently as yesterday." The anger was gone from Bob's voice. "If you're looking for something specific, I may be able to help."

"Oh, yes, sir. I'm well aware." The man in the windbreaker gave Bob an annoyed look and exchanged a few words with his female colleague. He started walking to the boardwalk.

"Careful with your steps there, please," Bob said.

"Do these stairs lead to your unit?" the windbreaker asked, looking up at Bob and pointing to the back stairs.

"They sure do. Come on up," Bob said.

Without thinking about the consequences, Bob unlocked and opened the balcony door that led to the back stairs. Pepper was out and down the stairs before Bob could stop him. The dog ran passed the cop and lifted his leg as soon as he reached the boardwalk.

"I'm sure the leash law applies to the Bay Ridge Condo property," the windbreaker said, with a slight smile, as he reached the landing outside Bob's door.

"Yeah, you're right," Bob said. "I opened the door to let you in and the dog took it as a signal to go take a leak. He doesn't usually do that," Bob felt a need to tell a white lie.

"Well, he'll be wanting to do that every morning from now on," the cop said. He walked onto Bob's balcony with his right hand extended. "Detective Lieutenant Joe Lazecki."

"Bob Meissner."

Before they completed their handshake, Pepper was back, seeking the attention and affection of the detective.

"Hey, little fella," Lazecki said. Reaching into his jacket pocket, he pulled out a medium-sized dog treat and held it up to Bob. "Okay to give him one of these?"

"I hate to reward his bad behavior, but, sure, go ahead. You'll have a friend for life."

"That's why I carry them everywhere I go," Lazecki said. "A real estate agent friend of mine taught me that trick years ago."

"Come on in, Detective Lieutenant Joe Lazecki. Would you like a cup of coffee?"

"That would be great. Thanks."

Bob handed him an empty cup, pointed him to the coffee maker, and advised that he would be back in a minute.

Bob changed out of his pajamas and into a pair of jeans and a tee shirt, and returned before the detective had taken his first sip of coffee.

"Sorry about my rough greeting, Detective. People will tell you that I'm pretty protective of the dune," Bob said, as they sat at the dining room table.

"Oh, they already have," Lazecki responded. "Your neighbor, Carol Walsh, stopped us when we arrived and told us you were the person to talk with for anything having to do with the dune. She said you're known as The

Commodore."

Bob made a slightly dismissive face at The Commodore reference.

"Then, Jerry and Gail Sandler stepped out of their condo on the first floor…"

"I know Carol and I know Jerry and Gail. Good people."

"And the Sandlers know you. They also told me The Commodore was the expert when it comes to this dune."

"Detective, I prefer to be known as Bob, just Bob. Now, I have to admit you have me more curious than before. Is there some way I can be helpful and maybe keep your well-meaning colleagues from doing more damage than they have already done to the dune."

"First, Bob, tell me what you were doing in the dune yesterday," Lazecki said.

"Keeping the dune healthy is something I care about a lot, Lieutenant. It's what keeps this place from being flooded in a storm. Every so often, I go into the dune to look for damage caused by careless kids, dumb adults, and, from now on, well-meaning cops."

"You do this alone?"

"Not all the time, but yesterday, yes, I walked through alone."

"And when was this?"

"Oh, mid-afternoon. 2:00 or 3:00, I suppose."

"Before dinner?" Lazecki asked.

"Oh, yeah. Well before dinner."

"And what were you looking for, Bob?"

"Nothing in particular." He decided not to share too much with Lazecki until he knew more. "It was a decent day, weather-wise, and I hadn't done a walk-through in a while."

Lazecki made a note or two throughout their conversation, but he didn't display a high degree of interest in what Bob had told him thus far.

"Okay, my turn. What exactly are you and your folks looking for, Lieutenant?"

"The easy answer is evidence. As you might have seen from your balcony, in addition to the crime scene tape, there's a tarp there in the dune. And it…"

"Oh, no," Bob interjected, knowing exactly what Lazecki meant.

"I'm afraid so. A lady out for a run on the beach with her dog found a body early this morning. Actually, her dog found the body."

Bob stood and went quickly to the balcony. He left the door open as he stepped outside.

"That's not a large tarp, Lieutenant," Bob said, after looking down into the dune. "From here, it looks pretty flat. Has the body already been taken away?"

"No. There's still a body there," Lazecki said from his seat in the dining room. We're waiting on the coroner. It's probably the angle from here that makes it look flat."

Bob doubted Lazecki's explanation. As he reentered the condo, he decided to press for more information.

"Do you know who it is?" Bob asked. He tried to maintain an even tone, but he was becoming anxious about the victim's identity.

"Not yet. Again, when you said you had been in the dune as recently as yesterday, I was hoping you might have some idea."

"I didn't see anyone in there yesterday. It's still spring. It isn't until the summer months that I have to run people out of there."

Bob was afraid his increased level of nervousness might be obvious to the lieutenant. Thoughts that it might be Malia's body lying in the dune nearly panicked him.

"Lieutenant, can you tell me if the victim was young, old, male, female?"

Lazecki didn't respond right away. Instead, he fingered his phone.

"I'll do better than that. If you're up to it, I'll show you the individual's face. It's not the prettiest picture you'll ever see. I have it on my phone, though."

"Sure, I'll take a look." In the short time it took the lieutenant to enlarge the photo so that only the face filled the screen, Bob focused on his choice of the word *prettiest*. He prepared himself to look at the face of Malia, dead in the dune.

Devlin's face was only slightly elongated. It had essentially returned to its normal shape and showed only a minor sign of the grotesque stretching that had occurred the night before.

"Are his eyes really that red or is that a reflection in the photo?"

"No. They're blood red. Have you seen him around here, Bob?"

Bob drank from his coffee cup and exhaled audibly. He looked down and slowly drew three fingers across the furrows of his forehead.

"Yes, Lieutenant. I'm sorry to say I know the young man. I met him yesterday. His name is Devlin." Bob paused. "You know, I can't recall his last name. I was told it, I'm sure, but I can't remember what it is. I'm sorry."

"Where did you meet him?"

"Right here."

"In the dune? I thought you said…"

"No. Not in the dune. He was here with his friend. A young girl. They go to the high school down there on North Great Neck."

"Cox High?"

"Yeah. That's it. Cox High School. They're seniors. She's visited a few times since I chased her out of the dune earlier in the week."

"What was *she* doing in the dune?" Lazecki asked.

"She told me she was walking on the beach and decided to wander into the dune. She couldn't say why or what drew her in, but I ran her out as soon as I noticed her from my lanai."

"Your what?"

"Lanai. My lanai," Bob said. Hawaiians call a balcony or a patio a…. You know what, never mind."

The words were coming more slowly to Bob now. He didn't realize it, but he was speaking so softly it was as though he had forgotten he and Lazecki were having a conversation.

Lazecki could tell Bob was grieving in a way. He didn't want to interrupt whatever internal musings might be vocalized. He simply leaned in across the table top to hear better.

"Oh, Christ," Bob said, lifting his head, making direct eye contact with Lazecki. "I may be the reason Devlin is dead."

"Okay, Commodore…Bob…there's clearly more to this story and I think it's time you told me all about it."

"Yes. I suppose you're right."

"Mr. Meissner, I feel obliged to advise you of your rights against self-incrimination."

"What? Oh, no need for that, Lieutenant. That isn't

what I meant when I said I may be the reason he's dead."

"Bob, I hope this doesn't cause you to stop talking to me, but I have to read you your rights."

"Oh, for God's sake, go ahead."

Lazecki gave Bob the standard warning heard so often on television police dramas. Bob sat impatiently drumming his fingers on the tabletop.

"You know, I have half a mind to throw your ass out of my home, Lieutenant. Remember, I invited you up here."

"I know. I apologize, but it was the right thing to do. Still feel like talking?"

"I've got nothing to hide," Bob said. He then told the detective about his first encounter with Malia, her subsequent visit with Devlin, and the cautionary tales he told them about the importance of the dune and the potential danger it represented.

"Did you dare them to go into the dune?"

"No. Of course not. I begged them to stay out of it and asked them to encourage their friends to stay out, as well."

"So, why would you think you're responsible?"

"Don't you see?" Bob said. "If I made the dune seem exotic or mysteriously attractive, it might have made going in there more tempting. He was just a kid, for God's sake."

"Bob, we'll talk to Malia. I'm sure she knows Devlin's last name," Lazecki said. "But I think we'll be able to get all the information we need at the high school."

"Malia drove him home yesterday. She'll know where he lives."

"Bob, you're right. There was no need for me to read you your rights. And I'll say it again, you can't blame yourself for what happened. Based on what you told me, you didn't do anything that would have reasonably caused the kid to go into the dune."

"Easy to say, Lieutenant. But I'll live with this for the rest of my days. Good news is I probably don't have that many days left."

Lazecki's phone rang. He responded with short answers to the information he was receiving. He then instructed the person on the other end of the phone to pursue the leads Bob had just provided.

"Get a car over to Cox High School. I want Malia Matthews sent to the principal's office as soon as she finishes her exam. If she isn't in school, get her complete contact information. I'm also willing to bet there is only one senior with the first name Devlin. That's D-E-V-L-I-N. Get his full name, address, etc. Find out how we can contact his parents during school hours. Yep. I think he's our John Doe. You have his photo on your phone, right? If you have to, show the photo to the principal, but I would rather you have the school show you a photo of the kid so you can see if it's a match."

While Lazecki was on the phone, Bob considered how much additional information he wanted to share at this point. It was obvious the lieutenant would be talking to Malia. She would probably tell him about the stories Bob shared. Bob couldn't know how much Devlin had shared with his parents. Bob also thought about Tony.

Tony was sure to be interviewed, along with Mary, Carol, Bo, Jerry and Gail, and God knows who else. If Tony had any doubts about Bob's mental stability, it would almost certainly come out. Bob wondered if it wouldn't be better for him to talk about it before Tony put a different spin on things.

The phone conversation over, Bob decided to see how receptive Lazecki might be to additional information of an unconventional nature.

"They've taken the body to the morgue. I'll be going

there soon," Lazecki said.

"You know, Lieutenant, there are a lot of stories about the dune and the unexplained things that have happened in there."

"Oh, I know. That's probably the thickest folder I've got in my desk. In fact, I have a box of folders on this topic. The stories go back years to when this place was a flea-bag motel."

"Probably before then, I would bet," Bob added.

A brief silence followed, as though Lazecki knew Bob had more to say on the subject.

"Well, Bob, I'm pretty sure we'll be talking again," Lazecki broke the silence. "Thanks for the coffee, but I have to get to the high school and eventually give Devlin's parents the bad news."

"Lieutenant, can I have just a little more of your time?"

Lazecki sat down again and held his hands out, palms up.

"I'm all ears, Bob."

"Lieutenant, I didn't tell Malia and Devlin those sea stories to scare them or give them bullshit they could share with their friends."

"Okay," Lazecki said.

Bob paused. "This is difficult to articulate without sounding as though I've lost my mind. I tried it with a friend of mine and I'm convinced he wants to have me committed."

"Bob, I'm going to have to ask you to get to the point. I have to reach out to the kid's parents."

"I understand. Of course. I'm sorry."

"Just say what's on your mind."

"Lieutenant, I don't know why, but for the last week or so, I've had a sense that something really awful is going on in the dune. I hesitate to call it unnatural, but I am convinced it's bad. Really bad."

"A sense? What does that mean, exactly?"

"Exactly. Good word. I've been asking myself the same question. This is where my good friend began to think my elevator no longer goes to the top floor. Lieutenant, I know that dune out there. I've heard the stories—many of which are probably in that folder you have in your desk. Something has been different lately. When I sit on my lanai, I can feel it. It's as though something that was asleep has awakened. Something that was satisfied is now hungry. It's the atmosphere that hangs over the dune. It's like it has a force it is giving off. A negative force. And then, the opening appeared."

"The what?" Lazecki asked.

"I noticed a hole in the dune a few days ago. It's an opening about yo big." Bob motioned with his hands indicating an area roughly twelve inches round.

"Bob, I don't have to tell you animals dig into dunes all the time. I'll bet that place out there is pretty active almost every night."

"That's what my buddy, Tony, said. His place is downstairs on the second floor. I'm not convinced that's it, Lieutenant. The opening appeared in a matter of seconds, and when it did, it was perfectly formed, as though it had been there for a long time."

"Don't you mean it was perfectly formed when you finally noticed it? Isn't that right?"

"No. It wasn't there. I went to the door to let Tony in and, when I returned to the lanai, there it was. In fact, Tony saw it before I did. Haven't seen an animal go in or come out and I've been keeping a nearly nonstop vigil here."

"That's what you've got? A hole in the sand and a funny feeling in your gut?" Lazecki asked.

"And, then, there's the coaler."

Bob told Lazecki when he first noticed the coal ship, and how it disappears and reappears in an area of the Bay where it isn't supposed to sail, let alone sit at anchor. As he said the words *disappears* and *reappears*, Bob more fully appreciated how absurd his proposition sounded. He could only imagine the degree to which Lieutenant Lazecki now discounted this statement and, probably, everything Bob had said up to this point.

"I don't know, Bob. And from those bits of information, you conclude what? There are evil spirits in the dune?"

"Well, Lieutenant, that theory is actually not without precedent, but I don't think you have the time or the disposition for me to…"

"Bob, it's been good talking to you." They shook hands. "You've been helpful, and like I said, I'll be back in touch with you."

As the lieutenant stood and turned from the table, Bob began to stand.

"What was left of him?" Bob asked.

Lazecki stopped, but didn't turn back to Bob.

"What's that?"

"I asked how much of his body was in the dune."

"His remains were intact. If you're asking if an animal got to him, it doesn't appear so."

Bob now walked around the dining room table and faced Lazecki.

"I'm asking about his insides—his skeleton and his internal organs. Was all that normal looking? Don't bother answering. I can tell by the hesitation in your voice and the expression on your face that I probably already know the answer. I'll see you out, Lieutenant."

They walked to the front door.

"Mr. Meissner. Commodore," Lazecki said as he paused at the door.

"Bob."

"Bob, I'm going to ask the coroner to give you a call. I think the two of you should talk."

"The coroner? Don't you mean the department's psychiatrist?"

"Bob, you may be a lot of things, but crazy is not one of them. Expect a call."

19

Devlin's father had noticed the light from the basement TV in the morning, but Devlin accurately predicted the way in which his parents would react. Both husband and wife left for work at their regular times. Mrs. Pryor left a note for Devlin, telling him to enjoy his day off and reminding him to eat a good breakfast by either scrambling some eggs or having a bowl of cereal.

When Lazecki met with Devlin's father, the man stared in disbelief. He called home. No answer. He called Devlin's cell. No answer. He left his office and drove home to find the house empty. The television in the basement was still on. The back door was unlocked. At that point, he drove to his wife's workplace. Together, following Lazecki's instructions, they went to the coroner's office where they were met by Lazecki and Dr. Arthur Zippeaux, the Virginia Beach Coroner.

"Mr. and Mrs. Pryor, because we do not yet have a cause of death," Lazecki said, "Dr. Zippeaux insists on limiting the number of people who come in direct contact with your son's remains. Please don't read any hidden message into that. There isn't one. It's simply policy. By limiting access to the body for a short time, we will be better able to determine the cause."

Lazecki was being less than honest with Devlin's parents. The police were not ready for them to see the condition of the boy's body. Lazecki was hopeful that, in the next day, the coroner would be able to determine how Devlin's skeletal structure and internal organs had seemingly vanished and he would have a substantive narrative to share with the Pryors.

"Now, sir…ma'am, when you are ready, I will ask the doctor to open the blinds. Devlin will be in a hospital bed. The bed will be adjusted to a partially sitting position."

"Lieutenant, you sound sure it's our son," Mrs. Pryor said. "My husband and I still hold out hope the poor soul on the other side of that window is someone other than Devlin."

"Isn't there a chance that's the case?" Devlin's father asked.

"I'm so sorry. Of course there's a chance, but you both need to be prepared for the worst, while continuing to hope for the best," Lazecki said.

Devlin's mother had been barely holding back tears since they arrived, but she began to sob uncontrollably immediately after Lazecki asked through the intercom for the blinds to be opened.

Devlin's father embraced his wife and began to cry. He nodded to Lazecki.

"Thank you, Doctor," Lazecki said.

The blinds were closed.

"I'll leave you two alone for a few minutes. There's no hurry. Take as long as you need. I'll be in the hall, just outside the door, when you're ready to go home. I'm terribly sorry for your loss."

"Lieutenant," Mrs. Pryor said. "Please have the blinds opened again so we can spend a few minutes with our son."

"Of course. I'll take care of that myself. I'll be in the hall if you need me."

Lazecki left the Pryors in the viewing room. He walked next door to ensure nothing had been done to Devlin's remains that would reveal the condition of his body. Then, he asked Dr. Zippeaux to reopen the blinds.

From the hall, Lazecki could hear Mrs. Pryor's crying

subside after three or four minutes. He guessed they were composing themselves as best they could before leaving the viewing room. When the door opened, Lazecki was surprised the Pryors didn't exit. Instead, Mr. Pryor asked him to rejoin them. Mrs. Pryor stared through the window at Devlin. She had one hand pressed against the glass.

"Lieutenant, this is all happening so fast," Devlin's father said. "Please tell us again when and where Devlin was found, who found him, and why we can't begin planning his … funeral?"

Lazecki again provided them with the facts he had regarding the dune, the jogger, and her dog. He remained intentionally vague about the release of Devlin's body. Lazecki was well aware he was walking a fine line between the police desire to withhold from the public any possible signature of the killer and denying the next-of-kin information (and the remains) to which they were entitled. He also knew that, at this point, he was simply unable to explain what actually happened to Devlin's body.

"Mr. and Mrs. Pryor, there is no reason for you to delay contacting the funeral home of your choice, consulting with clergy, and making appropriate plans. I may have given you the wrong impression about the delay. The doctor will conduct his tests and analysis and release Devlin's body very soon. Unless we find something I am certainly not expecting, we're talking as soon as tomorrow," Lazecki said.

"Tomorrow is Saturday, Lieutenant," Mr. Pryor said.

"I know this is new to you, but Dr. Zippeaux's staff and the area funeral directors are very experienced in the dignified and respectful transfer of remains from this office to the funeral home of your choice. Any funeral director will know how to contact the coroner. The fact that it's a weekend will not slow the process, I assure you."

Lazecki often shifted roles from detective to ad hoc family counselor in situations like this, especially when the death of a child was involved. In their conversation, Lazecki learned all four of Devlin's grandparents were still living and that Mr. and Mrs. Pryor had no experience dealing with the death or funeral arrangements of a close relative. Not surprisingly, Lazecki also found himself reassuring the Pryors that they bore no responsibility for Devlin's death.

"Mr. Pryor, I know it's difficult to accept, but nothing you could have done would have made a difference here. It appears Devlin had decided to leave the house without either of you knowing it. And the coroner estimates the time of death somewhere around two or three in the morning," Lazecki said. He knew his words could help only marginally.

"You're probably right, Lieutenant, but I still can't help thinking I could have done something."

"Mr. and Mrs. Pryor, go home. Console each other. Call your priest, minister, or rabbi. They can help. They can also assist in the selection of a funeral home. Take a few minutes together. I'm sure there are relatives and friends you need to notify and who can be supportive."

"I've already spoken to our next door neighbor on the way over here." Mrs. Pryor said.

"I can have someone drive you home if you'd like," Lazecki said.

"No. That won't be necessary. I'm okay to drive," Devlin's father said.

With that, the Pryors went home. They were overwhelmed when a handful of close friends and neighbors met them in their front yard to grieve with them and to help them begin the slow healing process.

20

Bob was surprised when the coroner himself telephoned early Friday afternoon.

"Commodore Meissner," his tone was all business. "I'm not sure how you might be of help, but Lieutenant Lazecki thinks we should meet in my office to discuss the recent death in the dune, which I understand is directly behind your home."

"Doctor, please call me Bob. The Commodore thing is a bit overplayed. Frankly, I'm not sure how I can help either, but I'm willing to do whatever I can. I know you are a busy man. When you identify an opening in your calendar, let me know. I'm pretty sure I can make myself available."

"Oh, no, sir. The lieutenant thinks we should meet as soon as possible. I would have called you sooner, but the young man's parents were here for some time. Can you come here today? Now?"

"Give me the address. I'll walk my dog and be there in less than a half hour," Bob said.

A glass wall separated the coroner's office from the reception area. When Bob arrived, Lieutenant Lazecki waved him in, but the door opened before Bob reached it.

"Commodore, I'm Dr. Art Zippeaux. We spoke earlier." They shook hands. "I believe you know Lieutenant Lazecki."

"Yes indeed, Doctor. The lieutenant and I met this morning when I was still in my pajamas," Bob said.

Bob declined the administrative assistant's offer of a cup of coffee and asked, instead, for a glass of water. He sat down across from Lazecki and Zippeaux.

"Bob," Lazecki began. "I decided it might be worthwhile to invite you here when you asked me about the condition of Devlin Pryor's body this morning."

"Pryor. That's it!" Bob said. He looked at the other two, who were clearly not prepared for the interruption. "Sorry," he said. "I've been trying to remember Devlin's last name since we spoke this morning."

"Bob, why did you ask me that question?"

Bob thought briefly about how to frame his response. He decided to be as direct as possible, even if it caused them to think he was crazy.

"Lieutenant, I told you about my sense that something very bad is going on in the dune."

"Your sense that something bad is going on? I deal in facts and science, Commodore," Dr. Zippeaux interrupted.

"Bob. Please, call me Bob," Bob said.

"I'm under a good bit of pressure to determine what killed this young man. Feelings and intuition have very little to do with my methodology."

"I understand, Doctor," Bob started to respond.

"Art," Lazecki spoke up. "I'm interested in hearing what Bob has to say. I think we can afford a few minutes to hear him out."

"Very well," Zippeaux said, in a voice lacking all enthusiasm. "Please continue, Commodore."

"Thanks. This will only take a minute. And, please, it's Bob."

Bob took a bottle of water from Zippeaux's admin assistant and, after a brief drink, began again.

"Doctor, I told the lieutenant that I had been in the dune yesterday for a brief period of time. Why? Because of the sense I already mentioned. A few days ago, I noticed the appearance of an opening in the dune's surface. When I saw absolutely no evidence of animal activity, I decided to get a closer look. The experience I had was frightening. I can get into that later, if you'd like, but…"

"Bob, before you get off on a tangent, please tell us what made you ask about the condition of Devlin's body," Lazecki's interruption was inspired by Dr. Zippeaux's obvious growing impatience.

"I'm about to get to that," Bob said. "When I was in the dune yesterday, I saw Shadow, the cat that belongs to a lady in our community."

"How insightful," Dr. Zippeaux could no longer restrain his cynicism. Bob ignored him.

"Shadow was dead. His blood red eyes appeared to be staring at me. With the exception of his skull, his body was no more than a pelt. Skin and hair, but no obvious skeleton and no blood."

Zippeaux crossed his legs uncomfortably and turned his head to Lazecki, who was already looking in the coroner's direction.

"I see," the doctor said. "Go on."

"Go on?" Bob repeated. "Go on where? That's it. I think there's something bad going on in the dune. I see a dead cat in an inexplicable physical condition. Then, I have an encounter with an opening in the dune—a friggin hole in the sand—that scares the living shit out of me. And then, you find Devlin dead the next day and I wonder if his body might not look like the cat's. Why? Because, as unscientific as it might sound, Doctor, I have the sense that something very bad is going on in the damn dune."

"Bob," Lazecki said. "I think we should go to the morgue."

"Oh my God," Bob said when he saw the pale, lifeless face of Devlin Pryor.

Although he had seen the photo on Lazecki's phone, the striking difference between this and the vibrant young man he met the day before stunned him. Bob had seen death before. He was with both his parents, at their bedsides, when they passed away. And he had been with sailors killed in combat or in training mishaps.

But here on the coroner's table was Devlin Pryor. A sheet covered him from his chin down. His face seemed nearly translucent which made it impossible for Bob to miss the red of Devlin's eyes beneath his closed lids.

Dr. Zippeaux looked at Lazecki, who nodded in reply. Zippeaux slowly removed the sheet, exposing what was left of Devlin.

It was the image of Shadow the cat that raised Bob's suspicions and caused him to ask Lazecki about the condition of Devlin's remains. But the sight of a human being in the same condition left Bob almost without breath. It was all he could do to keep from gagging. His stomach knotted at the sight of Devlin's skin lying flat on the stainless steel table.

There was no hint of a skeletal structure within. No obvious presence of organs. Devlin had been reduced to a human head atop an empty suit of skin.

"The poor kid," Bob said. "Is there any way to know if he was dead before this happened? I hope he didn't suffer."

"I have no way of knowing for certain," Dr. Zippeaux said. "But I suspect he suffered greatly."

"Careful, Doctor. I wouldn't want you to speculate," Bob said, giving the coroner a look of disdain. "That wouldn't be very scientific of you."

Lazecki felt the tension immediately and spoke without hesitation.

"Doc, please show Mr. Meissner the others."

"Others?" Bob asked. "There are others?"

The coroner moved across the room and pulled on the handle of an unmarked drawer about midway in a wall of similar drawers designed to hold cadavers. Bob followed Lazecki's silent invitation to join him as they stepped over to where Dr. Zippeaux stood. Bob was relieved when he saw the drawer did not contain a human corpse. Instead, three pieces of white linen covered three objects.

"You're familiar with Shadow," Dr. Zippeaux said, as he removed the cloth from the dead cat Bob had encountered in the dune.

"Joan Mulligan's cat. Of course," Bob said.

"She almost certainly thinks her cat ran off and we intend to let her continue to hope it will eventually come home," Lazecki said.

"The lieutenant said you told him you've been keeping a close eye on the dune for about a week," Zippeaux said.

"That's right," Bob answered.

"Well, probably a day or two before you correctly sensed the need to begin watching, these two fellows were pulled out of the dune by the crew on a trash truck."

With those words, Zippeaux removed the linens covering two additional animal carcasses. One was a cocker spaniel and the other a fox. Both were empty fur suits with intact heads. When he and Bob made eye contact, the doctor nodded as a silent acknowledgment to Bob's intuition.

Bob looked down at the animals. Six red eyes stared vacantly at him in death.

"What the hell is going on?" Bob asked.

"I wish we knew," Lazecki said. "I'm willing to bet the trash truck crew has picked up a few more of these carcasses without noticing or reporting on their condition. We've advised the FBI and told them we're willing to collaborate … if the Bureau has any interest or if there are any similar case files at the Fed level. No response yet, but I'm beginning to think we'd be better off calling in an exorcist."

"Amen to that," Bob said.

"Sadly, we cannot explain what is happening," Dr. Zippeaux said. "I must, however, acknowledge, Commodore—I'm sorry, Bob—that your intuition about the general area of the dune is unfortunately and inexplicably correct."

"His parents are going to have a hard time when they see the condition of his body," Bob said.

"I think we'll be able to avoid that," Lazecki said.

"Oh? How?" Bob asked.

"Today or tomorrow," Zippeaux began, "I'll get a call from the funeral director the Pryors identify. I'll work with that director to make the young man look as normal as possible. I wouldn't say it's routine, but funeral directors have instruments and devices to essentially fabricate an individual's skeletal structure. It's done when the deceased is crushed to death, has a catastrophic fall, or is in a really bad car accident. When the body is fully clothed, there is no evidence of the reconstructive effort."

"I'm hoping we will have the time to figure out who or what did this to him before we get that phone call," Lazecki said.

"Sounds like a long shot," Bob said.

"It's one hell of a long shot, Bob. We're still at ground zero on theories."

"And you thought I would be more helpful than I have been," Bob said.

Dr. Zippeaux nodded his head in agreement with Bob, but Lazecki was more considerate.

"Bob, you told us what you know. That's all I could ask for. I was willing to trust your discretion by showing you our cards. I was confident you wouldn't hold anything back."

A wall phone in the morgue rang. The coroner excused himself to take the call.

"Yes. I see. Okay. I'll be right up and I'll return the call," Dr. Zippeaux said.

"Well, gentlemen, so much for having more time," Dr. Zippeaux said, as he began to cover the three dead animals. "My assistant tells me Montgomery Funeral Home just called about Devlin. I know the owner, Vince Patton, very well. He's good at what he does and he's a great guy. I'll ask Vince to come along when he sends a team to take possession of the body. To be frank, I really don't think Devlin's body is going to tell us anything more than we already know."

"Art, we'll let you get back to work. Thanks for taking the time with us," Lazecki said.

"Doctor, it was nice meeting you despite the circumstances," Bob said.

"Commodore Bob, it was my pleasure. And I apologize for our rough beginning."

The three exited the morgue together and rode the elevator from the basement to the first floor. Dr. Zippeaux went to his office. Lazecki and Bob walked slowly in the other direction, toward the front doors of the building.

"I feel terrible about Devlin, Lieutenant. He and Malia essentially saved my life and I turn around and play a hand in getting him killed."

"Bob, I told you before—you had no role in that kid's death. It's a tragedy for sure, but it's not your fault."

"It's just awful."

"Now, you said he and Malia saved your life. What did you mean by that?"

Bob looked around the lobby of the building. The small waiting area, consisting of a sofa and two stuffed chairs, was unoccupied. There was a moderate amount of foot traffic in the lobby, but everyone he saw appeared to be walking purposefully and with little to no regard for the people around them.

"Got a minute?" Bob asked Lazecki. "Let's sit over there and I'll tell you a story you may have trouble believing."

As they walked to the waiting area, Lazecki said, "After today, it will be hard to come up with something I can't believe."

In the fifteen minutes that followed, Bob told Lazecki about the coaler and the charred walking stick.

"And then, just when I thought whatever is in the opening was going to kick my ass, Malia calls from the boardwalk."

"No kidding?" Lazecki said. Bob had his full attention.

"Timing is everything. So, while the two kids didn't get between me and the source of danger, I'm comfortable saying Malia and Devlin saved my life. If they didn't show up, it could just as easily have been my wrinkled, old carcass laying flat on the coroner's table," Bob concluded.

"Well, there's no guarantee you would have suffered the same fate, but I get your point, Bob. Maybe I should deputize you, so the two of us can go in there together after whatever the hell it is," Lazecki said.

"That's just what you need—an old fart like me as your backup," Bob said.

"Hey, I could do a lot worse. For the time being, at least, I'm going to have the area roped off with crime scene tape attached to some orange traffic cones."

"Ordinarily, Lieutenant, I would argue against that because it might only serve to tempt the curious to wander into the dune. But we're dealing with a killer, and I don't think you would be able to stand the heat if another person is killed and you hadn't declared the area off limits."

"Thanks, Bob. I know I'm asking the obvious, but I would like you to keep your eyes open for anything out of the ordinary."

They exchanged cell phone numbers and exited the building together.

"If nothing happens for a while," Lazecki said as they shook hands in the parking lot, "I'm afraid Devlin's death is going to be officially considered a freak attack by a rabid animal and his file will be added to the other Mysterious Dune Reports folder in my desk."

Bob checked his watch.

"Lieutenant, I have to get home. I have a dog in my condo who is probably about to have a shit explosion in my living room. But, if you have the time and the interest, I have a theory or two about all this that might not seem all that crazy after what you have seen today. Next time you're in the area, knock on my door."

"Why am I not surprised you have a theory about all this?" Lazecki said. "I still have to talk with anybody who was in your building last night. So, I'll be by tomorrow or the next day. I'll give you a shout."

"Our public servants working the weekend. Here comes a tax increase!" Bob joked. "See you soon, Lieutenant."

"Oh, and Bob," Lazecki said as they turned to go to their respective cars. "Stay out of the dune, please."

"Count on it, Lieutenant. Count on it."

21

"Where the hell have you been?"

"Well, it's nice to see you as well, Tony," Bob said.

"We started hearing that someone was killed in the dune. I naturally assumed it was you under the police tarp. But someone said it was a young boy. Then, I decided the police arrested you, but I noticed your car was gone. I was going to call the cops, but Mary said it would only turn you into a suspect." Tony's anxiety-induced speech was rushed, almost breathless. His concern for Bob was sincere.

Bob and Tony stood on the sidewalk of Page Avenue. Tony was there to check his mailbox. Bob took Pepper for a long-overdue walk as soon as he got home. He checked for his mail, as well.

"Tony, my paisano, you know you would have been my designated phone call if the police arrested me," Bob said. "Who needs a lawyer when I have you?"

"I'm serious, Bob. Mary and I were worried about you. And, just in case you've forgotten, let me remind you that this is not my original heart." Tony motioned to his chest.

"Stop it. Your heart is half your body's age. It can take a lot more than my being arrested. But, I know you're serious and I appreciate your concern. I really do. Tony, I'm fine. A body was found in the dune early this morning. You can relax. I'm not a suspect. In fact, I'm working with the police."

"How did *that* happen?"

"When the police questioned me about it this morning,

let's just say they were more interested in what I had to say about the dune than you have been."

"Hey, that's not a fair shot, but what made them come to you so quickly?"

"They're making the rounds. They'll be talking to everyone who lives in our building."

"Okay, but why did they go to you so soon?"

"I suppose they decided to talk to me when I tried to run them out of the dune."

"You tried to run them out of the dune?"

"The bastards woke me up and you know how I feel about people walking in the dune," Bob smiled at his friend.

They were now walking together in the parking lot, halfway between the sidewalk entry to the property and their building, when they spotted her.

"Commodore Bob. Oh, my God!" Malia yelled as she ran up to them. She hugged Bob tightly. "I was so worried about you when I heard the news about Devlin. Oh, Commodore, I'm so sad." Tears ran down her cheeks and onto Bob's shirt.

Malia might have continued hugging Bob were it not for Pepper's barking.

"I'm sorry, Pepper. I forgot to say hello to you." Malia was on one knee, trading affections with the dog.

"Uh, Bob," Tony said. "Is there something I ought to know about what's going on here?"

"Malia, meet Tony Castalano. Tony is my old friend. He lives at the Bay Ridge Condos part of the year and in Florida when it's too cold here for his delicate nature. He and his wife, Mary, are originally from New Jersey. Tony, meet Malia Matthews, the young lady you thought didn't exist."

"Didn't exist?" Malia said.

"Malia, it's a pleasure to meet you," Tony said. "I understand you and Bob met a few days ago."

"You told me, in so many words, that Malia was a figment of my imagination and that I believed she magically appeared out of the dune," Bob said.

"Well, it wasn't magic, but I kind of did come out of the dune when I met you, Commodore Bob," Malia said.

"See!" Tony added.

"That's not what she meant," Bob said, as he gave Tony a dismissive wave, signaling he was about to change the subject. "Malia, I'm so sorry. It's terrible news."

Malia lowered her head, unable to hide her sadness. She held a tissue to her eyes.

"What terrible news?" Tony said. "Wait. Is this about the body in the dune?"

This time, Bob had reached out to embrace Malia, who was trying hard to remain composed. Their lack of response to Tony's question was all the confirmation he needed.

"You both obviously knew the victim. How can I help?" Tony said.

The three of them began walking again toward Bob's building. Bob had a hand on Malia's back. She carried Pepper, who provided a wonderful distraction. As they walked, Bob retold Tony the story of meeting Malia and Devlin. He added the part about the police activity waking him in the morning and how the police had more than a passing interest in Bob's knowledge of the dune.

He intentionally omitted any reference to the condition of Devlin's body, Mrs. Mulligan's cat, and Lieutenant Lazecki's box of folders of unexplained incidents in and around the dune.

"Malia, you're welcome to come upstairs for an iced tea

or a Diet Pepsi."

"Actually, my dad told me I'm not allowed to go into your condo, but…"

"I didn't realize your father knew Bob so well," Tony couldn't resist the opportunity.

Malia laughed and said, "No, I was going to say that, under the circumstances, I would like to do that."

"I can bring you a drink down to the boardwalk, if you feel more comfortable," Bob said.

"No. Don't be silly, Commodore. I'm fine going upstairs."

"Tony, why don't you join us?"

"I'd be happy to."

"And, why don't you ask your lovely wife if she would like to come over? She's probably wondering where you are, anyway."

"I was wondering where you were," Mary said from the second floor walkway that ran the length of the building. She was unaware she had echoed Bob's words. "Hello, Bob. We were worried about you. Hello, young lady."

"So, I heard," Bob said, looking up at Mary.

"Hello," Malia responded almost simultaneously.

"Mary, we'll stop the elevator at 2 on the way up. Join us for a cup of coffee or a cold drink," Bob said.

"Malia, I've got to ask you to stop referring to this old fogey as Commodore. It goes to his head. Before you know it, he'll be parading around in the Navy uniform that he wore during the Civil War," Tony said, trying to lighten the mood a bit.

"I know, sir. He's told me I don't have to call him Commodore, but I think it's cute."

"Cute? Oh, brother."

"You really do enjoy breaking my chops, don't you?" Bob asked Tony.

"For sure. It's one of life's greatest pleasures," Tony said.

With that, there was a ping and the elevator door slid open on the second floor.

"What is one of life's greatest pleasures?" Mary asked, as she stepped onto the elevator.

"Oh, your husband's life would be incomplete if he couldn't give me a hard time," Bob said. "I don't know how he makes it through the winter when you're in Florida." Bob held his hand out toward Malia and continued. "Mary, let me introduce you to Malia Matthews."

Mary gave her husband a confused look as she held out her hand to Malia.

Bob went on, "I'm sure Tony told you about Malia, but he probably told you she was a product of my imagination and my failing mental capacity."

This time, Mary and Tony exchanged knowing looks.

It was a brief ride to the third floor, during which Pepper couldn't decide whether to give Mary or Malia the most attention. Bob had not locked his front door when he took Pepper for his walk. He invited them in.

"You have a really nice place, Commodore. But, you know, Devlin would have been disappointed," Malia said.

"Who's Devlin?" Mary asked Tony under her breath. Tony didn't respond.

"Disappointed? Why's that?" Bob asked.

"He thought you might have shrunken heads as souvenirs from an assignment in the South Pacific," she replied.

"Who's Devlin?" Mary asked, again in a voice only Tony

could hear. No response.

Bob laughed. "Sorry. No shrunken heads."

"Did you move the heads into the loft to hide them from the police?" Tony joked, pretending to look for them in the places they had previously been in the living room.

"Give the man a break, Tony," Mary said. "While Bob is getting drinks, tell me what's going on."

Tony recapped the day's events to the extent he knew them. Malia explained how she came to meet Bob and how much she enjoyed hearing his stories. For his part, Bob would add a detail or make a correction from the kitchen, or as he delivered drinks. He joined them in the living room with a can of Diet Pepsi in his hand.

"Well, this has been a pleasant conversation so far," Bob began. "And, Mary, it sounds as though you are all caught up. Although Malia mentioned his name, I think we have all skillfully avoided talking about poor Devlin Pryor."

"Who's that?" Mary asked, this time, loud enough to be heard by the group.

"The kid in the dune. I couldn't remember his name." It was Tony's turn to whisper. Mary wasn't sure she heard what he had said. But, before she could ask again, she heard Malia begin to cry softly.

"I'm sorry, Mary. I thought the knucklehead sitting next to you brought you up to date," Bob said. "Devlin Pryor is the young man who was found in the dune this morning by a lady who was jogging on the beach with her dog. It was the dog that alerted her to the body. Devlin was also a senior at Cox High School and was one of Malia's friends. I met Devlin the other day and I found him to be a respectful young man."

"I'm sorry I'm crying," Malia said. "But I feel it's my fault Devlin's dead. That's really why I came to see you, Commodore. I don't know what to do."

"Oh, honey," Mary said. "Why would you feel responsible for his death? I'm sure that's not the case."

"If it wasn't for me, Devlin wouldn't have known anything about the dune."

"Malia, it isn't your fault," Bob said.

"Oh, it is, Commodore. You don't understand."

"I understand better than you think, Malia," Bob said. "This morning, I told the police it was my fault Devlin is dead. After all, I told him about the dune. The truth is, none of us made him do what he did. In fact, he wandered into the dune despite my warning to stay out."

"Some things we know in our heads, but they're hard to accept in our hearts," Mary said. "Neither one of you should blame yourself."

"I hear you, but I should have stopped him. Even before you talked to us out on the boardwalk, he told me he wanted to go in to see what all the mystery was about," Malia said, emotion weighing on her voice. "Then, when I was driving him home, he told me he was going to explore in the dune. I tried to talk him out of it. Maybe I should have told his parents."

"Malia, you yourself just explained why you shouldn't blame yourself," Bob said. "Lieutenant Lazecki was right. He told me he was sure Devlin was determined to go into the dune at some point."

"But, I was in the dune the day you yelled at me..."

Tony and Mary both broke the somber mood by chuckling at Malia's comment. Bob smiled at their reaction and even Malia paused long enough to laugh slightly.

"Oh, I know I'm not the first person The Commodore has yelled at for being in the dune. But I was there and I wasn't attacked. I didn't even feel as though I was in danger."

"No, Malia. I don't think you were in danger. Whoever

or whatever killed Devlin, probably wasn't there when you were in the dune. Or, if it was there, it wasn't prepared to attack," Bob said. *And I didn't see the coaler that day!* Bob thought.

"So, what do you think, Bob?" Tony said. "What do the police think? Was it a person or an animal? Was it a random act?"

"Hell if I know," Bob said. "I have my theories, but everybody thinks I'm crazy."

"You're sounding saner and the world is sounding crazier every day, my friend," Tony said.

"Look, I'm no expert on this stuff."

"You're our local expert," Mary said.

"You know a lot more about the dune than we do," Tony said.

"About all kinds of dunes," Malia added.

"Okay, stop inflating my ego," Bob said, holding a hand up as if he were stopping traffic. "I read whatever I can get my hands on on the subject. The Internet is good and bad. Malia, as you found out, there's a lot of information out there, but some of it's junk."

"Our teachers always warned us about using the Web as a source," she said.

"There's a lot of folklore and legends that build over time around communities. And this is where my good friend, Tony, thinks I start wandering off the track. But I have to believe there's a thread of truth running through the fabric of all this. Enough truth to make me very concerned and very nervous about what might happen next," Bob said. "I don't know what else to say."

"Sure," Tony wouldn't let the conversation fall off. "But you're not saying every dune in the world is possessed, are you?"

"Possessed? Where'd you come up with that word? You're going to scare the kid," Mary said, motioning to Malia.

"No he isn't," Malia said.

"All right. You're scaring *me*," Mary said.

"I'm not sure that's the right word, but you're right. I think most coastal dunes are just dunes, doing their jobs protecting shorelines," Bob said. "I can't explain why, but our little dune seems to have a long history of strange things happening in and around it. Mary, you're the only one here who has been spared my stories."

"Oh, Tony has shared them with me, and when we first bought here, some of the ladies in the community talked about you, the dune, and your many stories," Mary said.

"I bet they had a lot to say about the loony guy on the third floor," Bob said.

Mary only smiled, silently confirming Bob's supposition.

"Lieutenant Lazecki tells me this isn't the first incident in our dune. They've drawn conclusions about some, but most have no explanation. Unsolved crimes, missing persons, downright bizarre incidents."

"You said they have a file?" Tony said. "I'm willing to bet it's more like a humongous drawer in a filing cabinet. Their info has to go back years," Tony said.

"Possibly," Bob said. He was still unwilling to share everything Lazecki had said about the police files.

"My only point is that this can't be the action of the same person if it's been going on for so many years," Tony added.

"Of course not," Bob said.

"And I can't believe there has been one animal or a pack of killer animals living in the dune all these years."

"That's not what I'm saying," Bob said.

"Wild animals don't attack only once or twice a year. Animals just don't behave that way," Tony concluded.

"Tony, you've said a mouthful, my friend. You may not even realize it, but much of what you just said has serious impact. And it's more than a little frightening," Bob said.

Tony looked at Bob, confirming he had been essentially thinking aloud. He hadn't given much thought to the conclusions implied by his words.

"You know what, folks?" Bob said, slapping his knees with his hands. "It's been a long day for me—for us. I'm going to hold off exploring my theories until I can give all this more thought."

"Really?" Tony said incredulously.

"Aw, Commodore," Malia added.

Once again, Bob held up a hand. "Wait. I do want to share a little more information about yesterday because I think it might help you feel better about yourself, Malia."

"What do you mean?" Malia asked.

"Malia, earlier today, I told the police that you and Devlin saved my life yesterday."

"I doubt that's true," Malia said.

Bob told the others about his journey into the dune on Thursday, his confrontation with the opening, and his sense he was about to be violently attacked in retribution for his assault on the dune. Bob didn't mention that he had seen the coaler in the Bay when he encountered the opening because he was still unsure about their relationship. But he was becoming increasingly convinced the presence of the coaler was an indication that the opening intended to feed on living prey.

"But then, you spoke to me from the boardwalk, Malia. And I'm convinced whatever was about to attack me, was less interested in having witnesses than in kicking my rear end." Bob's hyperbole was intended to console Malia.

"Hold on," Mary interrupted. "When did this happen?"

Bob told her.

"So, you were in the dune, talking to Malia—who was on the boardwalk," Mary said.

"Well, once I heard her voice, I began walking toward the boardwalk. But, yes, Malia was there."

"And so was Devlin," Malia added.

Mary playfully shoved her husband with both hands. He briefly leaned away from her on the couch, overplaying the force of her push.

"What?" Tony said.

"Don't you remember? That's when you told me Bob was standing in the dune, talking to himself. Did you look to see if there was anyone on the boardwalk?" Mary said.

"Come on. He looked like he was alone," Tony answered, smiling slightly, fully aware of his mistake.

"No, he's right, Mary. I was talking to my imaginary friends. In fact, right now, they happen to be on my lanai as we speak," Bob said with mock seriousness. "They're out there smoking imaginary cigars and drinking imaginary beers." He turned to his friend. "Thanks, Tony. Why didn't you call the mental health folks to come cart me away immediately?"

"I did, but they were too busy yesterday," Tony said, not-so-subtly giving his friend the finger, barely hidden from Mary and Malia by his other hand.

"Thanks. I love you, too," Bob said, returning the gesture with a broad smile. Malia giggled.

"Okay, children," Mary said to Bob and Tony. "Let's get back to your story, Bob. So, you honestly believe there was—maybe still is—something in the dune that killed Devlin, that almost killed you, and that is responsible for the death of many others for years or maybe decades?"

"So, if you don't care about preserving the shoreline, ladies and gentlemen, here's another reason to stay out of the dune," Bob said, as his way of giving Mary a positive response.

"I never thought I would say this about you, Bob, but don't you think you're being a bit too cavalier? If you're right, this really isn't a laughing matter," Mary said.

"Oh, you're spot on, Mary," Bob replied. "The truth is I'm forcing myself to sound upbeat. But, inside, this is driving me crazy."

"If that kind of information gets out in any credible way, our property values will crash," Tony said.

"I'm beginning to think we ought to leave the opening and the dune alone," Mary said.

"But, if we do that, it wins," Malia said. "Whatever is in the dune has done bad things. It really needs to be punished. It killed my friend and was about to get you, Commodore. You said you think it's killed a lot of other people. It makes me furious."

"I feel the same way, Malia," Bob said. "But we can't let our anger make us do anything stupid. You understand what I'm talking about, right?"

Bob paused before continuing. He hoped Malia would respond positively. Instead, she remained silent and looked away.

"I'm not worried about property values and I don't think the police are either," Bob continued. "At first, I thought the police wanted to avoid being ridiculed by the news media, but I've come to think they are afraid there would be panic all around the area if the things we've been talking about got into the newspapers. I'm going to be talking with the lieutenant tomorrow or Sunday. I should know more about all this by the end of the weekend. I'm still hoping I can get the police to act somehow."

A short moment of silence followed as everyone seemed to be absorbing what Bob was suggesting.

"Well, on that somber note," Mary said. "I think Bob is right. It's time to call it a day. Bob, please assure me you have no intention of going into the dune any time soon."

"Mary, I'm probably going to take a shower and go to bed. I'm tempted to put on the ballgame, but I'm afraid I'll end up spending the night in my recliner."

"Yeah, you've done that more than once this week, haven't you?" Tony said.

"True. I'll put the game on in the bedroom and fall asleep long before it's over, but at least I'll be in bed."

They stood to leave. Tony and Bob shook hands with a promise to get together in the morning. Mary hugged Bob and suggested he join them for dinner the next day.

"Rather than have you cook, why don't the three of us go somewhere? Malia, you're certainly welcome to join us, but I think our conversation would bore you to tears," Bob said.

Malia only smiled, betraying the awkwardness of a teenager who doesn't know how to skillfully decline an invitation from an adult.

"Are you kidding?" Tony said. "Her father doesn't want her seen in public with the likes of you, Mr. Big Shot Commodore."

"You know, that's not a bad idea," Mary said, completely ignoring her husband's latest dig at Bob. "There's a place I've wanted to try. What's it called, Tony?"

"The restaurant? Oh, jeez. There was an article in the paper about it the other day. What the hell is it called?" Tony said.

"Oh, right," Bob said, recalling the article. "*The Upper Room.*"

"That's it!" Mary said. "I'll call to make a reservation. I'll let you know the time," she told Bob.

"Sounds good, Mary. And dinner is on me," Bob said.

Bob gave Malia a hug.

"Go home, sweet girl. Stop blaming yourself. There is no reason for you to feel guilty. In fact, you should be proud because I honestly believe you saved my life."

"Oh, Commodore Bob, you're the one who saved my life. Whoever or whatever is in that dune is evil and I really want to see it punished."

Bob placed his hands on the upper part of Malia's arms, just below her shoulders. He looked directly into her eyes.

"Malia, don't get any crazy ideas. Evil can be tempting and I know you want revenge, but we aren't strong enough to face it alone. Not you. Not me. None of us. That's a lesson we all have to learn from Devlin."

She hugged Bob again and planted a kiss on his cheek. When she said goodbye and thanked him again, Bob was struck by a sense of finality. Every other time Malia left Bob, she promised to return. Not this time. Bob was confident her casual walks through the dune were a thing of the past and he recognized she would be off to college soon. So, it was only logical to consider it likely he might not see Malia again.

"Malia, remember, I'm always here if you need someone to talk to."

Malia smiled and nodded before she turned to go. It was obvious she was struggling to hold back tears.

22

When the front door closed behind Malia, Bob realized that, for the first time in many hours, he was alone. Pepper was there, of course, but in nearly every way, he had come to consider Pepper an extension of himself.

Bob sat in his recliner, physically and emotionally drained from the day's events. At first, he welcomed the quiet, but it soon allowed entry to an unsettling feeling of loneliness.

Being alone was never an issue for Bob. He never married. He missed the camaraderie of the Navy. Although, throughout his active service—when he wasn't at sea—Bob chose to live solo, never sharing with roommates the rent on a larger apartment.

He had a normal, healthy social life, but was always more comfortable with a single living arrangement. He had never considered himself to be lonely until now. Prior to his naval service, Bob thought about studying for the priesthood. Educated by the Jesuits, he knew a true religious vocation would steer him to that order. Eventually, he chose to serve in a military uniform, rather than a Roman collar. He never regretted his choice, but, every now and then, he wondered if his decision to remain a bachelor was a subconscious way of keeping his career options open.

He used the remote to turn on the evening news, but he hardly heard a word. His mind filled with the memory of Devlin. His heart ached for Devlin's family and for the life cut short.

Lost in his thoughts, Bob was surprised by the sensation of a tear moving down his cheek. He considered himself a compassionate person, but crying was not something he did easily—if at all.

Bob remained in the recliner for hours. He had no sense of the news broadcast transitioning to the standard network programming he routinely characterized as ridiculous and unwatchable. Tonight, they played in their entirety to a sleeping dog on the couch and a totally inattentive, troubled man.

In fact, Bob didn't exit his distracted state until the eleven o'clock news came on the air. He chuckled slightly when he realized how long he had been mentally elsewhere.

"Okay, Pepper, time to call it a day. Let's go for a quick walk."

They rode the elevator, cut through the parking lot, and walked briefly along Page Avenue. Throughout, Bob tried to recall the content of his nearly five hour hiatus in the recliner.

He remembered agonizing over the pain Devlin must have endured. He wished he could have changed places with him. The memory actually gave Bob a distinct ache in his stomach. He wondered how many others the dune would entrap and whether he would encounter the opening again.

I wonder if it is going to be dormant for a while, he thought.

This was the theory he hoped to discuss with Lieutenant Lazecki tomorrow.

Picking up after Pepper and meeting a neighbor on the same mission with her dog gave Bob welcome relief from his introspection. When he and Pepper reentered the condo, Bob had only sleep on his mind.

He decided to forego the shower and, when he went to bed, sleep came surprisingly fast. His expectation was that he would spend a good bit of time staring at the ceiling, reliving all that had happened since he was awakened by the police. He was happy to be wrong.

That night, Bob's sleep was deep and dreamless.

*Do not be conquered by evil,
but conquer evil with good.*

Romans 12:21

Saturday

23

It was nearly 9:30 when Bob awoke on Saturday morning. Sitting on the side of the bed, he wondered if the events of the day before might have been a bad dream.

That hopeful note was shattered when he stepped onto the balcony to allow Pepper to sneak down the back stairs and return promptly when the deed was done. The presence of the crime scene tape instantly told Bob all he experienced on Friday was very real.

"Damn," was all he said as he leaned forward, his fingers intertwined and his forearms resting on the balcony railing.

Bob stared into the dune. He had a sudden realization that explained fully the sense of loneliness and the feeling of unease he experienced the night before. He had unfinished business in the dune.

He feared there would be no victory over the evil that so clearly remained alive in there. Its appetite appeared to be invigorated at unpredictable intervals. It amazed him that so many couldn't (or wouldn't) see the danger for what it was.

I wish it didn't have to be me, Bob thought. *And it'll probably kill me. But, I've got to do what I've got to do.*

"You may be the only part of me that remains when I'm gone," Bob said to Pepper, who barked once in reply. "Damned if I don't think you understand what I'm saying most of the time."

Turning back to the dune, focused on the spot where the opening had been, Bob said, "Are you too shy to be seen, you evil, old bastard? Does the police tape embarrass you? Too much attention? Or have you had your fill for now?"

No opening in the dune and no coaler in the Bay, Bob thought. *Is it gone or just resting between meals?*

"Bastard. Evil bastard," Bob spoke again to the spot where the opening had been and, he was convinced, would be again. "Let's get some breakfast, Pepper."

Bob was hungry and he felt like cooking. He decided a big breakfast at this hour of the morning, with no more than a handful or two of peanuts later in the day, would hold him until his planned dinner out with Tony and Mary.

Bob prepared a huge western omelet, fried a portion of breakfast potatoes, cooked a half dozen strips of bacon, and toasted two slices of wheat bread. Pepper eagerly consumed anything Bob tossed to him. Together, Bob and Pepper ate like kings.

"Pepper, that was a two-cup-of-coffee meal," Bob said, patting his stomach.

Breakfast cleanup would be followed by household chores neglected during the week. There were clothes to be washed, vacuuming to be done, and the weekly bathroom once-over. After that, or perhaps before he got to all of it, Bob hoped Lieutenant Lazecki would visit as promised.

"Lots to do today, little dog," Bob said. "But first, let's get you out for a good walk."

As he and Pepper exited the elevator and began walking through the parking lot to Page Avenue, Bob spotted Lazecki getting out of his sedan parked in a visitor's spot.

"Hey, Lieutenant, my door's not locked. Feel free to let yourself in. We'll be back in a minute," Bob said.

"Not just yet, Bob," Lazecki said. "I'm still making the rounds in the complex. I just went out for a cup of coffee and an egg sandwich."

Bob and Lazecki closed the distance between them.

"I wish I had known. I just ate breakfast and would

have gladly fed you."

"No problem. Don't want the neighbors to think I'm reporting to you about them," Lazecki said.

"I get it, but I do expect a full report, you know." Bob smiled and turned to continue through the parking lot with Pepper. He stopped again when Lazecki continued talking.

"I don't think I'll be more than another hour—two at the most. By the way, it probably won't surprise you to learn that nearly everyone claims to have seen or heard nothing out of the ordinary. The first they knew anything was going on was when they saw cops in the dune. And everyone continues to tell me that you are the man to see if I have any questions about the dune."

"I'm not surprised," Bob said.

"And more than one suggested you might be a little out of touch with reality," Lazecki added with a smile.

"That doesn't surprise me either, but how is it we all—myself included—missed the sounds of a kid suffering and dying in the dune?"

"Remember, it wasn't exactly a quiet night. There was a hell of a storm Thursday night."

"I suppose you're right," Bob said.

"I'll see you in a couple of hours."

In addition to Pepper's walk, Bob managed to get all of his domestic chores done, and still no Lieutenant Lazecki. Lazecki's time estimate proved to be understated by an additional two hours. It was 3:30 when he rang Bob's doorbell.

"Long day?" Bob said, as he invited Lazecki in. "Beer?"

"That's tempting, Bob, but I'll stick to a Diet Coke or Diet Pepsi, if you have it."

"Coming right up."

"These things always run over, but today went way longer than I expected," Lazecki said. "After I saw you in the parking lot, I interviewed a slew of people, from your building and the others, who wanted to explain in great detail that they had nothing useful to tell me."

"Lieutenant, I don't want to extend an already over-extended Saturday workday for you," Bob said.

"Bob, I told you I was interested in whatever theories you have about all this and I meant it. I know some of the people in the Bay Ridge Condominiums think you're a little, let's say, out there." (Lazecki made air quote signs with his fingers.) "But, let's face it, *out there* is a kind way to describe this case and the many others in the files I told you about."

"I appreciate that. You know, I should have asked you this a long time ago, but do you want me to call you Lieutenant or Detective?"

"At this point, Bob, I'd appreciate it if you called me Joe."

"Absolutely. Thanks."

"You know, we can talk here or, if you want, we can go get a pizza," Lazecki said.

Bob explained that he and the Castalanos were going to dinner. Realizing Lazecki was hungry, he put out a bowl of pretzels, crackers, and a block of cheese. Lazecki was not shy about helping himself.

"I'll listen to whatever you want to say, Bob, but I would like to know if you really believe you weren't attacked because Malia Matthews and Devlin Pryor showed up."

"I don't really know the reason, but I don't think keeping two teenagers from witnessing my tortured death is enough motivation for whatever is in that opening to cancel its plans. No, I think it was pissed at me for sure. Hell, I even saw the coaler while I was in there. For some reason, it decided not to attack. Maybe it didn't think I was worth the effort."

"What do you mean, you even saw the coaler?"

"I think there's a relationship between the coaler and the opening."

"You do?"

"Joe, this is going to sound crazier than anything you've heard so far. I think the coaler shows up when the opening intends to attack. Or, just maybe, it's the other way around. You know, the coaler appears when it wants the opening to go into attack mode. Suppose whatever it is in the opening sucks the life out of its victims and then sends their souls to the coaler?"

"Do you know what you're saying, Bob? Do you realize what something like that means?"

"I'm still coming to grips with the idea. In fact, I'm trying to talk myself out of it. Maybe, when it got a whiff of me, it decided my old bones and guts are not flavorful enough. Or, maybe, it just has no use for old men."

"Are you just saying that to keep me from eating these snacks?" Lazecki said.

"I think it would take more than that to get a cop to lose his appetite. Anyway, back to your question, for a while, I thought it was the kids who saved me. That was my initial reaction. I even told Malia that yesterday because she was so down on herself."

"I want to get back to your weighty theory in a minute, but why was she so down on herself?"

"She thought she was responsible for Devlin's death."

"Where have I heard that before?" Lazecki asked rhetorically.

"She's an emotional kid who's been through a lot. She's angry as hell with whatever is in the dune. She wants it punished."

"You don't think she'll do something stupid, do you?"

"Don't know, but I doubt it. She's a smart kid. I think she respects the danger. Hell, it killed her friend."

"It's the old battle between logic and emotion. Keep an eye on her, Bob," Lazecki said.

"Well, she'll be off to college before summer ends. Frankly, I'm not sure she'll come around here again," Bob said.

"I wouldn't be so sure about that. It's clear you're important to her."

"Either way, I'm concerned about her and anyone else who might wander into the dune. You know, whatever plans you have for the dune will have a bearing on the likelihood of it hurting people in the future," Bob said.

"So, you don't think it's done?" Lazecki asked.

"How could it be? You told me yourself that you have cases going back decades with no closure. Do any of them also have bodies in the condition we found Devlin or the animals?"

"I can't answer that," Lazecki began.

"Come on, Joe," Bob reacted. "I thought we were going to talk honestly and not BS each other."

"No. That's not it. You can come down to headquarters and I'd be happy to go through the files with you. I can't answer your question definitively because the case notes are not clear. In almost every case, there's reference to a body or a body part recovered. A lot of the cases refer to the body being in a severe case of decay or words like that."

"So, you're thinking there were others like Devlin, but, whether to protect against future public disclosure or because they didn't know what the hell they were dealing with, the words used are vague, at best?" Bob said.

"At best," Lazecki echoed. "What I do know is that I can't keep that part of the dune taped off forever. Besides, the tape might draw more attention than just leaving it unmarked."

"Wouldn't that be great? The city or the state might not be liable to the families of future victims, but I don't think you or I would be able to get a good night's sleep for the rest of our lives," Bob said.

"You're right, of course, but I don't know what to do. I've thought about recommending the city give the piece of beachfront to the Feds for them to fence off, but that would mean this place probably gets condemned under eminent domain."

"No way is that going to happen."

"Of course not," Lazecki said.

"What about going into the opening with a miniature, mobile camera?"

"You know, I thought of that. I asked that very question to the Chief of Detectives. He said cost wouldn't be an issue, but he thinks the department and the city would send me for a series of psychiatric tests and then they would disapprove the request because of the media attention it would draw."

"Oh, for God's sake, Joe. Are you serious?"

"As a heart attack, Bob. The Chief of Ds said it would start a thousand rumors and that the rumors are always worse than the truth."

"Maybe not in this case." Immediately after saying that, Bob held up a hand. "Wait," he said. "Did you hear something?"

"No. What was it?" Lazecki asked.

"Not sure, but I thought I heard someone calling my name. Man, I must have had too much caffeine today. My head is beginning to ache."

"Are you okay, Bob?"

"Yeah. I'm fine. Just hearing things and getting a strange pain in my head. It's probably that I'm getting hungry. Don't worry about it, Joe. It'll pass." Bob didn't want to lose his train of thought. "I don't think there's a chance of turning the land over to the Federal Government. You can float the idea if you want, but nobody—not the city, the state, or the Feds will take you (or me) seriously. Do you have anything else in mind?"

"I have one idea that I think might work, but it requires me to do something radical."

"How do you mean?"

"Well, if I can find an advocate, I would try to get the city and the Army Corps of Engineers to announce a collaborative test of flood prevention, advanced drainage technology, or dune preservation techniques. I really don't care what they call it. They would designate this area of the dune as the test site."

"And?"

"And the Corps of Engineers digs into the place until they confront the problem or find themselves knocking on the doors of hell," Lazecki said.

"Don't laugh," Bob said. "I agree that's pretty radical, but what are the odds you'll be able to find an advocate?"

"That's actually not the radical part, Bob. The radical part for me, is that I would have to retire from the force before I would feel comfortable openly pushing for something like that. The odds of success? Slim to none. But like you said, I want to be able to sleep at night without feeling the weight of the lives of any additional victims on my conscience."

"Joe, I'm not going to be around much longer, but I'm willing to help in any way possible. When I'm gone, little Pepper will still be here. Maybe he'll be able to inspire you to keep up the fight." Bob said as he responded to Pepper's request to have his belly scratched.

"You're not going anywhere any time soon, my friend," Lazecki said.

"I don't know about that, but, if you have a little more time, I'll share the rest of my theory with you, if you're interested."

"That's why I'm here. Shoot."

"I think we've established that we have a big problem on our hands. Bigger than anything you've probably imagined to this point. To sum it up in a couple of words, Joe, I think we are dealing with pure evil there in the dune."

"Pure evil? It sounds to me like you're talking about the Devil."

"If that's how you describe pure evil, so be it. The bottom line is that I don't care what you call it. I think it's real and it's worse than anything you or I could imagine. Why in my dune? I have no idea. But I think it's been there for a very long time—hundreds, if not thousands, of years. No way to tell if this is the only place on the planet where this is the case. Maybe it is and maybe it isn't. Again, I have no idea why our dune is its fertile ground, but it's hard to deny something terrible is going on."

"Go on," Lazecki said.

"Here's where it gets even stranger. I think it goes dormant in between. I don't know why it stops attacking and I have no idea what causes it to start up again. But I think this would help explain the intervals between incidents in your files."

"Bob, what you're saying is incredible. I don't have any better theories, but, you're right, yours is extreme. Let's say you're right, what's the solution?"

"That's just it. I have no idea. Stay out of the dune and

I think you're safe. I don't think there are any reports of people being attacked in this way outside the dune."

"None that I know of."

"Something about it entices people to go to it, but it's at their own peril."

"So, what do we do, put up signs telling people if they value their lives, they'll stay the hell out of the dune?" Lazecki said.

"That would get some attention, wouldn't it?" Bob laughed. "Actually, I've thought about this and I think the first thing to do is to post signs on the edge of the dune. They'd urge people not to endanger the eco-structure, or some term like that. The signs might even say the dune could be dangerous."

"Do you have any idea how long it would take the city to approve signs like that?" Lazecki said. "Two budget cycles, at least."

"I'll tell you what. If you can help ensure no one from the city takes them down, I'll have the signs made on my dime."

"You do that and I will—unofficially, of course—get some steel posts from the traffic division. We can mount the suckers and I'll help you put them on the border of the dune between the two bayfront buildings and the Bay," Lazecki said.

"You've got a deal. Adequate warning. No public panic."

"And, if you disregard the signs," Lazecki began, "you're screwed!"

"This will save some lives, but not all. And that's why it's only the first step. Without the next step—and maybe even with it—people will still wander in and the police will retrieve the pelts of human beings who fell victim to whatever the hell it is," Bob said.

"I suppose that's why it's called free will," Lazecki said.

"I guess you can say that," Bob said. "But we both know THOU SHALT NOT ENTER! sign posts aren't enough. You and I, and maybe people who come after us, are going to have to confront that son-of-a-bitch directly."

"I'm afraid planning for our next step is going to have to wait for our next meeting, Bob. I just saw what time it is," Lazecki said. "I've got to get going and I know you're going out to dinner. I'm serious about those signs. You get them made and I'll come up with the hardware and the volunteer manpower to get them in the ground permanently, with cement footings."

The two men stood and shook hands. They started walking toward Bob's front door.

"So, can I rely on you to tell my neighbors I am not insane?" Bob asked.

"Gee, Bob, I don't know. I may be willing to fight the Devil with you, but now you're asking the impossible."

"Thanks, pal."

"I know you really don't care what they think. Truth be told, I think you're a long way from crazy. Either that, or you have infected me with your nuttiness."

Bob opened the door and that's when they heard it.

24

The scream filled Bob's condo unit as though it originated simultaneously in every room. The two men looked at each other, both knowing the hairs on their arms and the backs of their necks were on end.

"What the…"

"It's from the dune!" Bob said.

Another scream.

"It sounded like a female," Lazecki said. "God, I hope it's not Malia!"

"I bet it was her voice I heard," Bob said.

The nervousness and concern in their voices was obvious and growing. When they exited Bob's condo, Lazecki stepped across the open front walkway to the elevator and pressed the *Down* button.

"No time, Joe," Bob said and began moving along the walkway to the stairs. Lazecki followed, impressed that Bob moved more quickly and with more agility than he would have expected for a man his age. They had descended just beyond the second floor by the time they heard the elevator ping, indicating it had arrived on the third floor.

Good call, Lazecki thought.

Bob and Lazecki hustled through the pool deck, but were surprised that there wasn't a heightened level of activity among the handful of people at the pool.

Hadn't they heard the scream?

Lazecki recognized Sara Fowke, one of the last residents

with whom he met earlier in the day.

"Could you tell where the scream came from?" he asked.

"I didn't hear a scream," Sara said.

"We didn't hear any screams either," Dick and Gayle, neighbors from the other bayfront building, said in unison.

Lazecki's face betrayed a degree of confusion, but he never stopped to explain or to get an explanation. Bob was already across the pool deck and through the second gate, moving along the boardwalk toward the rear of his unit.

It seemed clear no one on the beach or elsewhere in the community's property heard the scream that Bob was certain came from the dune.

Even before Bob reached the part of the boardwalk directly in line with his rear balcony, he knew he had been correct. Something was going on in the dune. He saw dune grass moving erratically and inconsistent with the direction of the light breeze. Lazecki closed the distance between them and they stopped almost simultaneously.

"There! Someone is in the dune," Lazecki said.

Together they left the boardwalk and made their way toward the activity. Someone was calling to Bob from behind, but Bob wasn't about to turn his back on the opening if it had, in fact, reappeared. Instinctively, Bob already knew it had.

"Bob, where are you going?" Tony happened to be looking left from his balcony when Bob and Lazecki came from the pool deck. He immediately decided to head down his back stairs, sensing the urgency in the movement of Bob and the detective.

Before he could call out a second time from the base of the stairs, Tony heard Bob's voice.

"It's Malia!" Bob said.

Bob and Lazecki paused only long enough to realize

Malia was in serious trouble. Acting on instinct, Lazecki grabbed Bob's arm the instant he made a movement to go to her.

"Hold on, Bob. Let's figure this out first," Lazecki said.

Malia was clearly resisting something that was drawing her forward. She was facing west with the beach and the Bay to her right. Bob and Lazecki were to her left.

She seemed to be trying to take small steps backward, but it was all she could do to keep from falling forward. At first, it looked as though she was bent forward at the waist, but Bob realized her torso and legs were nearly aligned. She was leaning forward from the ankles. Even her hair was pointing to what Bob knew was the opening in the dune. It certainly looked as though her feet would soon leave the ground as her body was pulled forward.

"No time," Bob said, as he broke free of Lazecki and ran toward Malia. He staggered when he reached her, but somehow found the strength to wrap his arms around her waist.

"I've got you," he managed to shout to her, nearly breathless. Although he and Lazecki heard no sounds when they stopped only feet away from Malia, Bob was now in the mix with her. It was as though they were inside sustained hurricane force winds and Bob knew he had to yell if Malia was going to hear him.

Malia struggled to say, "No, Commodore. Get away. It's Devlin. I saw him. He needs my help."

Bob's instinct was to survive, but, if he had time for coherent reflection, he likely would have admitted he fully expected to die and only hoped he would be able to throw Malia clear of the danger so that Lazecki could save her.

By this time, Tony had joined Lazecki on the periphery of the struggle. Lazecki recognized Tony as Bob's close friend who voiced concern for the old man's mental stability during their interview, but, in the midst of this, Lazecki couldn't recall Tony's name.

"I guess the old guy's not crazy, after all," Lazecki said, still breathing heavily.

"You've got that right," Tony said.

"Okay, I think the two of us need to get in there and wrap our arms around both of them. Let's treat whatever it is like a rip current. Do you know what I mean?" Lazecki said.

"I think so," Tony answered.

"Don't try to pull them back away from it. Instead, let's pull them sideways, back toward the boardwalk. That might get them out of the force of the pull their experiencing and keep us from getting sucked in, as well. It ain't great, but it's the only plan I've got."

"It's better than anything I could pull out of my ass right now. Let's go!" Tony replied.

As they stepped to join the fight, they heard Bob let out an enormous grunt. Actually, it was half grunt and half roar.

When they looked up, they saw Bob completing a kind of discus throw. He spun clockwise, and three-quarters of the way around, he released his hold on Malia. As he loosened his arms, he shoved her toward Lazecki and Tony. Although they wrapped their arms around her as soon as she was within reach, they couldn't keep her from falling to the ground. The three of them briefly rolled in the sand of the dune. But they were safe. Bob's move was successful.

"Are you okay, Malia?" Tony asked, when they disentangled themselves from each other.

There was no answer. Malia lay there on her back. Lazecki placed two fingers on Malia's neck and put his ear to her chest.

"I can't tell if she's alive or dead." Lazecki's own

breathing was so labored he was unable to feel a pulse or hear a heartbeat.

Tony reached in his pocket for his cell phone. It wasn't there. He quickly looked around and located it not far from where Malia lay.

"I'll call 9-1-1," Tony said.

"Once you get through to them, start CPR on her. I'm going to help Bob."

But it was too late.

When Lazecki stood to assist Bob, he realized the struggle had ended. It was quiet. There was no sign of Bob.

Lazecki drew his service pistol and walked slowly, nearing the site of the struggle Malia and Bob had with the unseen evil. He stopped when he was certain he had reached the precise spot as evidenced by the marks in the sand. He looked to the west and saw it.

The opening was there. Lazecki realized how well Bob had described it to him. He could see only a deep darkness within the hole. Pistol drawn, he moved cautiously toward the opening.

"Tony?" It was Mary's voice calling from the boardwalk.

"I'm fine," Tony said. "Go out front and guide the paramedics when they get here."

Lazecki recalled Bob's recounting of his first direct exposure to the opening and how he sensed it was poised to attack him. Lazecki had the same feeling now. At the first sign of a struggle with the thing, Lazecki planned to fire his entire clip and run. He only hoped he would still have the physical ability to run if all that happened.

Another step forward.

Nothing.

Lazecki stopped. From the corner of his eye, he

saw something, but he was unwilling to shift his focus completely from the opening. As Lazecki took a couple of small sidesteps he saw a shoe lying on the dune floor.

Crouching low, he holstered his gun and moved quickly to the shoe. At almost the same time, he realized the shoe was still being worn by its owner and the owner had shape and form.

Bob's head was lying on the sand. He was not conscious. Lazecki could see the sand around Bob's mouth and nose move slightly as he exhaled. He was alive.

"Hey, Tony," Lazecki yelled, having noted Tony's name when Mary called to him.

"You okay?" Tony asked.

"I'm fine. I'll need a clean pair of skivvies when we get out of here," Lazecki said.

"You and me both, man," Tony answered.

"Bob's alive, but we're going to need another ambulance."

"I figured at least one of us was going to get hurt. When I called, I told the operator we needed two ambulances."

"Smart man," Lazecki said. He turned his attention to trying to communicate with Bob, but it was a one-way conversation.

The sirens of the approaching ambulances got the attention of many in the Bay Ridge Condo community. A crowd gathered at the pool to watch the paramedics at work. However, no one noticed either the presence or the sudden disappearance of the coaler that had been lingering in the shadow of the Bridge-Tunnel. There was no bright light on the bridge this time as the coaler simply faded away.

25

From the moment they began attending to Malia in the dune, the EMTs knew hers was a life-threatening situation. They worked quickly and efficiently to stabilize her and prepare her to be transported to the hospital.

When the emergency room doctors saw her and realized there was no overstatement of her condition by the EMTs, Malia was rushed to an operating room. Her surgery lasted almost six hours. On two occasions, her blood pressure fell so dramatically the surgeons thought they were about to lose her.

Late Saturday night, one of the surgeons exited the surgical area and introduced himself to Malia's parents, whose collective high anxiety level was apparent on their faces.

"Mr. and Mrs. Matthews, I'm Dr. Christopher Williams. I'm one of the team of doctors and nurses who operated on your daughter."

"How is she, Doctor?" Mrs. Matthews asked.

"She's a strong, young woman. She made it through the surgery. I suspect you know as much as I do about how she was injured."

"Yes. Lieutenant Lazecki, from the Police Department, called us. He met us when we got to the ER and spoke with us when Malia was taken to surgery. We still have questions, but he gave us his card and promised to stay in touch," Mr. Matthews said.

"I'm sure he will. Malia is not out of the woods yet, but there's every reason to be hopeful," Dr. Williams said.

Malia's mother, no longer able to hold back her tears, buried her head in her husband's shoulder.

Dr. Williams waited for her to regain her composure. He wanted to be reasonably sure she would be able to comprehend what he told them.

"It was touch and go on several occasions, and more than once, I was afraid we might lose her," Dr. Williams continued. He put his hand on Mrs. Matthews' shoulder and continued, "I'm not telling you this to upset you any more than you already are. In fact, I think you should look at my words positively. Malia is a fighter. I am convinced she is determined to get well. She does have a broken leg, but it's been reset and placed in a cast. We are going to have to watch her very closely for the next few days because of her internal injuries, but I have every reason to think she will recover," he concluded.

"When can we see her, Doctor?"

"It won't be too long. In about ten or fifteen minutes, she'll be moved from the operating room to the intensive care unit. She'll be there for a few days or so. You can head there after I've answered any questions you might have. Let them know who you are. Visitors are pretty much restricted to adult members of the immediate family. That's to guard against the risk of infection."

"We understand," Mr. Matthews said.

"I'll check in on her in the morning and again tomorrow afternoon. If you're in her room or in the family waiting area when I see her, I'll gladly give you an update. If you have any questions, don't hesitate to ask. The ICU nurses are great and they know how to reach me, whether or not I'm in the house. Now, she's going to be a bit groggy when you see her. She may not even know you're there. Don't be discouraged. She's been through a lot and she's been sedated. Her improvement may be slow, but, if we're lucky, it will be steady."

"Doctor, the truth. Will our daughter recover fully?" Mr. Matthews asked.

"I can't answer that question right now. Her internal organs are functioning, but they were damaged. Some more severely than others. The human body has amazing regenerative qualities. We did remove her spleen, but that isn't a big deal. She had several broken ribs. Certain movements will give her discomfort as a result, but ribs heal on their own. It's also unclear how much of all this she'll remember, of course."

"Are you kidding? I doubt she will ever forget this experience," Mr. Matthews responded.

"Actually, I would expect her to remember very little about the experience. In fact, she may never fully recall what happened to her," Dr. Williams said.

"Well, she'll remember who we are, right?" Mrs. Matthews asked.

"Almost certainly, yes. But I'm obliged to advise you that there have been cases where a person's amnesia was long-term."

"Is it ever permanent?" Malia's father asked.

"My God," Mrs. Matthews said before Dr. Williams could answer. She again buried her head on her husband's shoulder.

"Mr. and Mrs. Matthews, it's way too early to jump to conclusions. Let's cross those bridges if we come to them," Dr. Williams said.

"But *can* it be permanent?" Mr. Matthews insisted.

"I don't think we'll be facing that eventuality, but there are cases where the patient's memory is restored with the exception of any recollection of the traumatic event." Dr. Williams hoped he would get away with intentionally avoiding to answer the question.

"In a way," Mrs. Matthews added. "That might be the best outcome we could hope for. There's no reason she has to live the rest of her life with this awful memory."

"I can understand why you might feel that way," Dr. Williams said. "But, keep in mind, if that happens, Malia would be aware there is a significant hole in her memory."

"Yes, but still," Mrs. Matthews said.

"Sometimes, the psychological implications are more significant than the physical," Dr. Williams said. "But, as I said, we're getting way ahead of ourselves. Let's see how she does in a day or so."

26

The hospital medical staff was impressed that, despite his advanced age, Bob suffered no broken bones. He was badly bruised from his encounter with the opening. He sprained his back muscles, probably when he threw Malia to safety.

From Lazecki's description of what had happened in the dune, the doctors were most concerned with the possibility of concussion. They were again surprised when Bob passed the tests. He showed no signs of concussion, barely had a headache, and had total recall of the events.

"Mr. Meissner, I'm Dr. Kris Maney."

"Nice to meet you, Doc." Bob tried unsuccessfully to hide his surprise that his attending physician was female. "I'm sure you're here to give me a report. I'd appreciate it if you skipped to the bottom line and told me when I can get out of here," Bob said.

"The nurses told me you were spunky," Dr. Maney said with a chuckle. "Tell you what, I'll start with the news you probably don't want to hear. I expect you will be here a week."

"Yeah, let me stop you there, Doc." Bob was intentionally using a tone that was not confrontational. "You see, I'm not a big fan of hospitals. Way too many sick people. A week is just too long."

"Mr. Meissner, I am certainly willing to see how things go each time I examine you, but I can't make any promises at this point. You took quite a beating and I want to be sure you're okay outside and inside before we let you go home."

"Okay, Doc. How about this, if you're open to me

going home as early as tomorrow, I'm willing to hear your thoughts every day," Bob said. He showed a twinge of pain as he shifted in the hospital bed.

Dr. Maney laughed. "Going home tomorrow isn't an option, Mr. Meissner. You have to understand that a man your age…"

"Bob."

"Excuse me?"

"Bob. Call me Bob. I'm not big on the Mr. Meissner thing. I figure when someone looks me in the eye and calls me Bob, it's probably harder for him or her to bullshit me. If you will excuse my French, ma'am."

"You'll only get the truth from me, Bob. I promise. You got banged up pretty severely as evidenced by the significant bruising, but, amazingly, there are no broken bones. Unfortunately, the blood tests indicate you suffered a relatively minor heart attack during the struggle."

"What does relatively minor heart attack mean exactly?" Bob asked.

"Well, to be blunt with you, Bob, at your age, it means you're still alive. Anything greater than relatively minor and…"

"I get it, Doc. You don't have to build me a watch. Just tell me what time it is. I'm still interested in going home as soon as possible."

"I understand. It isn't going to be tomorrow. You have to accept that."

"Minor heart attack. I got it. Don't exert yourself. I understand. Eat right. Will do. Another test or two tomorrow morning, and I figure I'm heading home right after lunch."

"How do you feel about nothing less than three days?" Dr. Maney said.

"Three days? You are trying to kill me, aren't you, Doc? Like I said, too many sick people are in hospitals. A hospital is the worst place for an old fart like me."

"Actually, you're not wrong about that, Bob." Dr. Maney appeared to be checking other information on Bob's chart. "I tell you what, I promise to get you out of here just as soon as it's medically prudent and as soon as the nursing staff can bear to go on without your charm and wit. You've already made quite an impression on them. I like your attitude. If you don't stress about being here, your attitude will help you go home sooner rather than later. And that, Bob, is no bullshit."

Bob chuckled at her use of his word. "Okay, Doc, you've got a deal." Bob extended his hand and they shook on it. Again, Bob winced in pain from the reach to shake hands.

On Monday morning, Dr. Maney told Bob things were looking good, but she definitely wanted him to spend a third night in the hospital.

"But, Doc, we had a deal," Bob said.

"We still have a deal, Bob," Dr. Maney replied. "I want to be convinced you have no internal injuries that haven't manifested yet. Give me one more night and I might be able to get you out of here around lunchtime tomorrow."

"Do I have a choice?"

"Not really," she said, smiling broadly, as she exited Bob's room.

For the remainder of the day on Monday and part of Tuesday morning, nurses, technicians, and a few random doctors put Bob through a series of tests and blood draws. Dr. Maney didn't get to Bob's room until 2:30 Tuesday afternoon.

"Really?" Dr. Maney stopped in the doorway when she saw Bob dressed in street clothes.

"You said lunchtime, Doc. Who eats lunch at 2:30?"

"I think I said 'early afternoon' or 'around lunchtime.' Don't get ahead of yourself, Bob. Remember, nothing happens unless you are medically ready to go home, regardless what I say *might* happen. But I think you're going to be happy with what I have to say."

"Yes. You're right, of course," Bob said. "I'm just anxious to get out of here."

"Well, Bob, all the tests indicate you're healthy as a horse. Albeit, an old horse who had a very rough day." She looked up and smiled at him. Bob returned the smile. "As I said, your test results are all good. I've contacted your primary care doctor's office. You have an appointment a week from today at 11:00 a.m." Dr. Maney handed Bob a sheet of paper from her prescription pad with the date and time of the appointment written on it. "If you can't make that time, call to reschedule, but I want you to see him for a follow-up no later than a week from today."

"I got it, Doc." Bob stood to leave. They shook hands. Dr. Maney did not let go.

"Not so fast, Bob." The doctor gave Bob several pill bottles. "Here are meds I want you to take. The instructions are on the bottles. Your primary care doc will reevaluate the need for the meds next week, but these will get you through until you see him. Don't go a day without taking the meds."

Dr. Maney talked Bob through each medication, why she prescribed it, and how often Bob was to take it.

"This is a lot to remember," Bob said.

"The instructions are on the labels and I've written them out on this sheet of paper. If you still think it's too much to manage, just climb back into bed. Our excellent nursing staff will be happy to ensure all medications are administered on time."

"You drive a hard bargain, Dr. Maney. I really do

understand what I need to do. Many thanks for putting up with me."

"I'll sign your discharge papers. The nurses will help you with the admin side of things. Take care of yourself, Bob."

Less than an hour later, Bob was in the passenger seat of Tony's car.

"You're crazy, you know that, right?" Tony said.

"That's not the first time you've said that about me, Paisano," Bob replied.

"I'm serious. Mary and I would gladly watch Pepper a few more days. You should have stayed in the hospital until you were fully recovered and as long as they were willing to keep you."

"Come on, Tony. Have we met?" Bob said.

"I know. Nobody keeps The Commodore down."

Bob rolled his eyes. "Thank God we're almost home."

Tony laughed slightly and turned the radio a bit louder, indicating he got Bob's message. It was time to change the subject or just shut up.

"Tony, do you know anything about Malia?" Bob said, after a minute or two without conversation. Tony immediately lowered the volume of the radio.

"Is she still in the hospital? How is she doing?" Bob continued.

"I was waiting for you to ask about her," Tony said.

"Oh. I asked about her every day in the hospital. I always got one of two answers. Either, 'patient information is private' or 'I'll try to find out and get back to you.' Of course, when they did get back to me, it was to tell me that patient information is private."

"I know she is still in the hospital. Lazecki is our only source of information on her. He has been by twice and he's been awful tight-lipped."

"Can't say I like the sounds of that," Bob said.

"Well, he has managed to keep it out of the news."

"I never thought about the media. Has there been any interest?"

"None so far that we can tell. Look, Bob, I don't know anything for sure, but I'm with you. I don't like the lack of info. I think Lazecki would be more chatty if she was okay. I'm just not sure."

Tony pulled into his parking space and cut off the engine.

"Thanks for the ride, Tony. Your driving is actually improving."

"Thanks, coach. You know, I would have gladly let you out at any red light or, frankly, anytime along the way, regardless of the car's speed. All you had to do was tell me you were dissatisfied with my chauffeuring skills."

"You know I'm not sure I'm up for driving just yet." Bob shifted quickly from joking to seriousness. "If you're not doing anything tomorrow or Thursday, do you think you could give me a ride to the hospital? I'd like to see her."

"It may be tough cancelling my lunch plans with the Pope, but I will do it for you."

"You're a prince."

"It might be smart to call Lazecki first. He might be more open with you than he has been with Mary and me," Tony said.

"Good idea."

Bob's reunion with Pepper was the highlight of the day. The happiness they both displayed was enough to bring a tear to Mary's eyes. Before Bob left to return to his condo, he again thanked Mary and Tony for the transportation and for watching Pepper. He tried unsuccessfully to talk Mary out of her promise to prepare his meals for no less than a week.

Though Bob would admit it to no one, the hospital discharge process and the ride home drained him of energy. He put a glass of water on his nightstand and stretched out on his bed fully clothed. When he awoke, it was evening.

Bob expected his extended nap would make it impossible for him to get a good night's sleep. After taking Pepper for a slow-paced walk, Bob was again tired. This time, he changed out of his street clothes, took the medication Dr. Maney prescribed, climbed between the sheets, and drifted off quickly.

27

Bob's sleep Tuesday night was somewhat restless. He woke without a full recollection of the content of his dreams, but he was certain he had dreamed of a confrontation in the dune. He wasn't sure if the dream was about his first encounter with the opening, his most recent struggle, or of a face-off yet to come. The dream would recur Tuesday.

Wednesday morning, he was about to pour cereal into a bowl when the doorbell rang.

"Who the hell is ringing the bell this early in the morning?" Bob said, as he exited the kitchen and headed for the front door.

Seeing the shadow through the smoked glass, Bob knew exactly who it was. He opened the door.

"Good morning, Mary."

"Hi, sweetie. I can't stay, but here's a bowl of oatmeal. Eat it now, before it gets cold. Then, eat the fruit. There's no grapefruit in the bowl because I know you shouldn't have grapefruit because of the meds you take. I'll pick these things up at noon, when I bring you your lunch."

"Mary, this is not necessary. I mean, I'm grateful, but I can make my own meals. Honest," Bob said.

"I'm not saying you can't," Mary answered. "I'm only saying you aren't going to cook for the rest of the week. We'll reassess the situation over the weekend."

"As I've said before, there is no point in arguing with you. By the way, why don't you reschedule the dinner we had to cancel? Some night this week would be great."

"Are you sure you're up for it?" Mary asked.

"For sure."

"You know, that's not a bad idea. I bet they're booked solid for Friday and Saturday by now. How about Thursday? That'll give you another day to regain some strength."

"Thursday sounds good," Bob said.

"Thursday. Dinner at the Upper Room. I'll call for a reservation and let you know our time when I come back with lunch," Mary said. "By the way, I'm taking my little sweet dog for his morning walk. I will bring him back to you at noon, as well."

"Thank you, mother," Bob said, as Mary hugged him and turned to leave.

"Don't forget to eat the oatmeal before it gets cold."

Not surprisingly, Bob sat down immediately and ate the oatmeal. He rinsed the bowl and then took the plate of cut fruit onto the balcony. He sat at the high table, slowly eating. He stared into the dune, formulating his next move with respect to the opening. Of this he was sure, there would be a next move and the move was going to be his.

After nearly two hours of silent contemplation, Bob stood and returned to the dining room table where he began drafting the content of the signs he promised Lazecki. He was confident he could find a graphic arts business willing and able to produce signs to the city's standards.

As far as Tony and Mary knew, Bob was maintaining a low-stress, recuperative routine since his discharge from the hospital. Without consulting Bob, Mary identified a group of neighbors from the community willing to check in on Bob to ensure he was not over-exerting himself. Beyond advising them to wait a day before they visited, either Mary failed to assign specific times for them to stop in (which would have been uncharacteristic of her) or the well-intentioned neighbors didn't pay a lot of attention to that particular directive (which was more likely).

Between 10:00 a.m. and 2:00 p.m. on Wednesday, Bob was visited by a dozen of his neighbors. Time he hoped to spend recuperating and thinking was, instead, shared with well-wishers he found himself hosting. In the middle of one visit, Mary delivered lunch. Bob was grateful Mary's delivery cut short that round of visitations. Soon, after lunch, the parade of friends and acquaintances began again. At 2:30, Bob called the Castalanos.

"Hello, Bob." Mary said when she answered the phone. "Is everything okay? Wait, I'll put you on speaker."

"Mary, I know you organized the flow of neighbors to check up on me, but…"

"Bob, I don't know what you're talking about," she lied.

From the background, Bob heard Tony's voice.

"Come on, Mary. He may be sick, but he isn't stupid."

"Mary, I'm grateful. I truly am," Bob said. "It's wonderful that the neighbors have me on their minds, but can you dial back the intensity a bit? So far today, almost twenty—count 'em—twenty people have 'stopped by' to see me because they were 'in the area.' (Bob's overstatement of the number was intentional.) I'm on the third floor, for God's sake. No one just happens to be on the third floor. If this keeps up, I'll need to hire an event planner."

"Okay. I'll take care of it. I suggested times when they should visit. I guess they didn't pay attention."

"Do you think you can call off the visits for the rest of the week? Frankly, they're exhausting."

"Bob, I'm so sorry. They were supposed to help you relax."

"Yeah. That's not happening."

"Consider it done. I will still bring food, but no one else will bother you."

"Thanks, but please be sure no one is offended. I really am grateful. I just need some space."

"I understand. I'll tell everyone that we'll begin again next week and I will stress that the visits have to be spaced out and coordinated."

"That's why I love you, Mary," Bob said.

"Hey!" Tony rejoined the conversation. "Mary's husband happens to be here with her and he can hear everything you're saying."

"Mary, when you are ready to dump the sluggard you're currently living with, give me a call," Bob said.

"Best offer I've had all day," Mary responded, playing along with the joke.

"Sluggard? If I knew what that word meant, I think I might be offended," Tony kept the joke alive.

They hung up. Bob was relieved the parade of visitors would be discontinued, at least temporarily.

28

Malia's condition improved steadily and without any setbacks. The Matthews were relieved to hear the doctors reassure them that Malia was definitely going to recover. By Tuesday, she was fully communicative with her parents, and, as Dr. Williams had suggested, the scope of her amnesia extended only to the incident in the dune.

Malia was not happy when her parents refused to tell her exactly what had happened. She knew she had been in some kind of accident, but, to this point, she had no recollection of being in the dune, of confronting the opening, or of the struggle that came close to killing her. She repeatedly told the doctors and her parents that The Commodore saved her, but she recalled no context.

The doctors advised Mr. and Mrs. Matthews not to fill in the gaps immediately.

"Often," Dr. Williams told them, "the brain will heal on its own and at its own pace. Research also suggests it will heal naturally to the degree healthiest for the individual. We see no signs of swelling. So, there's no reason to suspect she will have seizures. We'll continue to keep an eye on her for a while, but I'm going to move her from the ICU to a regular room. She's making remarkable progress."

Malia was thrilled to be able to have visitors. Several of her girlfriends appeared at the hospital on Thursday within an hour of learning she had been moved out of the ICU. Malia's parents saw their daughter's attitude brighten and Dr. Williams assured them the visits with friends would quicken her recovery.

At one point, there were four friends visiting. Malia's

parents told her they were going for a cup of coffee and to call a few relatives to bring them up to date on her recovery. About thirty minutes later, Malia's father saw the girls enter the hospital cafeteria to buy soft drinks.

"Honey," he said to his wife. "It looks like Malia's friends are on their way out. We ought to get back to her room."

When they walked down the hall, they were surprised to hear laughter coming from Malia's room. They recognized Malia's laugh and were heartened by it, but the sound of more than one male voice made them increase their pace.

"What the hell are you doing here?" Malia's father said, presumably to both men standing at the foot of Malia's bed.

Ignoring the tone of her father's voice, Lieutenant Lazecki responded with a big smile and, "Well, hello, Mr. and Mrs. Matthews. Good to see you. And isn't it great to see Malia looking so good?"

"Don't give me that. What are you doing here? And with him? You have some nerve," Mr. Matthews said.

"Excuse me?" Lazecki countered.

"If it wasn't for you and especially you," Mrs. Matthews pointed directly at Bob. "Our daughter wouldn't have almost died."

"Mother!" Malia said. Her heart and blood pressure monitors responded appropriately. "I'm not sure exactly what happened yet, but I know Commodore Bob is not to blame."

"Mrs. Matthews," Bob began. "No one feels worse than I do about what happened. I only..."

"You only *what*?" Malia's father spoke up. "You can't undo what's been done and you can't walk away from your responsibility for all this. I don't understand why you're not in jail right now, but don't think we aren't going to sue you for all you've got."

"Sue?" Malia said. "Daddy, what are you talking about?"

"Malia," her father responded. "I don't know what exactly this Svengali has done to you, but he's liable in a very big way."

"Mr. and Mrs. Matthews, please calm down," Lazecki said. "I've looked into the situation personally. Malia is correct. It was Mr. Meissner who cautioned Malia about the possible danger in the dune and it was Mr. Meissner who encouraged her and her friends to stay away. Remember, Malia had wandered into the dune before she even met Mr. Meissner. In fact, it was Bob who almost certainly saved her life by putting himself in danger the other day."

"I knew it," Malia said.

"Lieutenant, please!" Mrs. Matthews said, hoping to get him to stop talking about the incident in the dune.

"I have to know what happened to me," Malia said. "Commodore Bob, please tell me what happened."

"Malia!" her father said sharply.

"Malia," Bob said. "I have to respect your parents' position on this. Eventually, your memory will come back to you. I'm sorry my visit here upset them and you so much. That wasn't my intent. When I got out of the hospital and learned you were still here, I only wanted to visit to wish you well." Bob paused and seemed to be fighting the urge to cry. "I should go."

"Yes, you *should* go," Mr. Matthews said. "In fact, you can't get far enough away."

"You were in the hospital, too?" Malia said. "Oh, Commodore, am I the reason? Did I cause all this?" She began to cry.

"Come on, Joe," Bob said to Lazecki in a soft voice, as he started walking to the door. He couldn't remember a time in his life when he felt this sad. Bob carried his sadness with him to dinner with the Castalanos. He apologized for being such a poor dinner partner.

29

Friday began as had the other days since Bob got home from the hospital. Mary delivered breakfast and took Pepper on her way out the door, promising to return at noon.

Mary noticed that Bob didn't exchange his usual banter with her. She decided not to mention it because she knew there might be any number of reasons for his bad mood to have carried over from Thursday's dinner. She also considered he might be suffering from the effects of a poor night's sleep. She thought it most likely his wounds hurt more today than yesterday. The doctors told Bob he might experience more aches and pains as the healing progressed and that some days would be better than others. Bob shared that bit of information with Mary after he and Tony returned from the hospital. Of course, there was always a chance Bob was just in a grumpy mood.

Mary knew Bob well. She knew he cherished his privacy, and, if he wanted her to know something hurt more today than yesterday, he would tell her without any prompting.

Bob ate his breakfast, brewed a second cup of coffee, and carried it to the balcony. He was happy there would be no interruptions from his well-meaning neighbors. As he had done each day since his release from the hospital (when the neighbors weren't visiting), Bob sat on the balcony, intensely looking into the dune.

It was just before 11:00 a.m. His face frowned with displeasure when his cell phone rang, but his expression changed dramatically when he saw the caller ID.

"Well hello, Lieutenant Joe Lazecki. How the hell are you?"

"Never mind me. How are you doing?" Lazecki said.

"I'm fine, Joe. Thanks for asking." Bob replied.

"It sounds to me that you're trying hard to appear more upbeat than you really are."

"No. No worries, my friend. Really. It'll all work out. You have to have faith. I still have a few bumps and bruises, but, all things considered, I'm fine. I've been doing a lot of thinking and I'm pretty sure I know my next step."

"Do you still plan to order those signs for the dune?" Lazecki tried to divert Bob's attention.

"For sure. I've sketched out what I want them to look like. I'd like to run them by you before I place an order. I'll make a few phone calls and search the Web. By the time I'm out and about next week, I'm sure I will have identified someone who can produce a quality sign." Bob said.

"Do you have anything else planned for today?" Lazecki asked.

"Not really, I guess, but I can't sit still, Joe," Bob said. "Malia may be a kid, but she was right. Bad things are going to happen long after we're gone, but, if I'm not part of the solution, I'm part of the problem. I think I've come up with a novel approach. I'm just working on the best way to go about it."

"Bob, you're starting to worry me. I'm going to swing by your place. Just assure me you won't do anything dumb before I get there."

"Define dumb, exactly," Bob responded.

"I'll see you soon."

Lazecki hung up and went quickly from his desk at headquarters to his car. He was nervous for his new friend. He pushed the speed limit, but couldn't justify the use of lights and siren.

Wearing a pair of jeans and a *Virginia is for Lovers* tee

shirt, Bob Meissner exited the balcony of his condo. He carried his walking stick and he moved deliberately down the back stairway. He was so lost in his thoughts, that he nearly missed a step on a couple of occasions.

Wouldn't that be a hoot, Bob thought. *After steeling myself for an epic battle, I end up falling down the stairs, breaking my neck!*

The moment Bob entered the dune from the boardwalk, he sensed he was in the presence of evil.

"Well, this is a hell of a way to test a new theory," he said, as he stepped deeper into the dune, moving toward the location where the opening had been and, he would soon learn, had returned.

Walking carefully with the aid of his charred walking stick, Bob arrived at the small clearing in front of the opening. He turned to face the darkness within it. He felt a lukewarm draft on his face. He stood there motionless.

Without saying a word, Bob was confident he was communicating his message to whatever it was that lay within the opening. The draft in his face was now a stronger breeze whose temperature had increased to an uncomfortable level. Bob placed both hands on his walking stick and planted its end in front of him, giving himself a three-point stance in the sand, facing the opening.

The force of the column of air intensified. Bob had felt and observed the contradictory nature of it. A strong column of air blew directly at the opening's target (in this case, Bob), yet the target felt a here-to-for inescapable pull forward. The atmosphere around Bob was loud now, but he suspected no one else heard anything other than normal beach sounds.

The struggle continued. The column of hot air was intense, as was the force trying to pull Bob forward. Throughout, Bob stood silent, staring intensely into the opening, using his walking stick as a vital stabilizer. Despite the assault on his body, Bob maintained his motionless stance. Anyone seeing his face would conclude he was in some kind of trance.

Again, the force of the wind, its temperature, and the pull on Bob's body increased in severity. The noise was deafening. It reminded Bob of hurricanes he had experienced. It was as though he was in a capsule of turbulence. Outside the capsule, it was quiet. Those not experiencing the drama were completely unaware. Before too long, Bob assumed his ear drums would rupture, his skin would burn, and his internal organs and skeletal structure would be absorbed into the opening.

And then, it was calm.

Only then, did Bob show movement. It wasn't as though he returned suddenly from an unconscious condition. To the contrary, he turned very matter-of-factly, as though he had just completed a routine task. He turned to face the Bay. Looking through the blades of dune grass, he watched as a distant coaler drifted away and, in a wink, vanished.

A slight, satisfied smile creased Bob's face.

"Score one for the good guys," he said softly.

Without hesitation, he turned his back to the opening and began to walk toward the boardwalk. Bob climbed the back steps, and reaching the landing on the third floor, he began to feel the full physical impact of what he had just experienced.

Were it not for his walking stick, Bob might have fallen to his knees or worse, down the steps. He managed to open the door to his balcony. He moved slowly and sat heavily on his lounge chair before lifting his legs and lying down.

Bob knew he was spent. He was oddly aware that he was no longer fully present on the balcony. It was as though he was in a fog.

Is this what dying is like? he wondered.

He was sure he heard the doorbell, but he made no effort to stand. The bell rang again.

Elapsed time and the sequencing of events became less clear. There was a sense that Pepper was licking his hand. He might have heard Mary say, "Oh, my God."

There was a definite increase in activity. Was Tony at his side? *Are you checking my pulse, Paisano, or trying to hold hands?*

Then, there was a bit more clarity.

I must be coming out of it. Hey, is that you, Joe? I did it, man. I faced it down. Stood there like a rock. Used a three point stance. Didn't have to say a word. That must have driven it crazy. I knew I couldn't 'out-evil' it. You know what I did? I decided to 'out-good' the thing. I figured it was trying to get into my head. So, I kept thinking, 'Good wins. You lose.'

Lazecki looked up at Mary and Tony from his kneeling position at Bob's side.

"His hands and face are burned pretty badly, but he's still alive," Lazecki said. "Damn it! I knew he was going to go into the dune again."

"The ambulance ought to be here any minute," Tony said. "Carol Walsh is out front. She'll direct them here."

"Hang in there, Bob. Help is on the way," Lazecki said.

Mary now crouched at Bob's other side. She held his hand and brushed his hair with her free hand.

*Once you eliminate the impossible,
whatever remains, no matter how improbable,
must be the truth.*

Arthur Conan Doyle

Sunday

30

Only a day after her release from the hospital, Malia was nearly overwhelmed by the reception she received from the people at church. Their affection was genuine and their sense of relief sincere. She was a bit embarrassed when the pastor thanked God for Malia's recovery and the congregation followed his comments with sustained applause.

After the family returned home, Malia asked if she could join some of her friends at the nearby Bagel Baker on North Great Neck Road. Since she was not yet cleared by the doctors, Malia's friend, Mags, agreed to drive. As Mags pulled away from the curb in front of the Matthews' home, Malia asked Mags for a big favor.

"Mags, are you willing to do something important for me?"

"Yeah, sure. What?" Mags said.

"Before we go to the Bagel Baker, can we make a stop?"

"Where?"

"Just up Shore Drive. I want to stop in on Commodore Bob to see how he's doing and to apologize for the way my parents treated him when I was in the hospital."

"Will they be okay with this?" Mags asked.

"Not a chance. My dad told The Commodore he was responsible for what happened to me and that we're going to sue him."

"So, maybe we shouldn't go see him."

"Mags, I have to apologize. I felt so sorry for him when

he left the hospital. It was terrible. I was embarrassed and angry when I saw how awful my folks talked to him. And that includes my mother."

"Okay, but I …"

"It'll just be a quick stop. I promise," Malia said.

"Do you think I can meet him?" Mags asked.

"Sure. I don't see why not. As long as he's feeling okay, of course."

They drove along Shore Drive and, after two quick turns, were in front of the Bay Ridge Condominium gates on Page Avenue. Mags found a parking space on the street. Malia suggested they use the public access pathway and walk along the beach in the direction of Bob's condo unit.

They proceeded very slowly. Mags carried Malia's lone shoe, as well as her own pair.

"Walking on crutches in the sand can't be easy," Mags said.

"It's harder than I thought it would be, but I'll be fine. It's not all that much farther. In fact, that's The Commodore's balcony right up there," Malia said. "He calls it a lanai because he used to live in Hawaii."

"Isn't that where you were born?" Mags asked.

"Right. That's sort of how he and I started talking. After he chased me out of the dune, of course," Malia laughed slightly. "If we're lucky, we'll see him leaning on the railing with Pepper nearby."

"Just be sure you don't get any sand inside your cast," Mags said. "Your parents will kill me, for sure."

The girls paid little attention to anyone else who might have been on the beach. They continued to stare at the balcony as they walked.

"Hello, my young friend."

They stopped. Both girls shifted their focus from the balcony to see Bob standing in front of them on the beach.

"Commodore Bob!" Malia said. She freed her arms to hug him by placing her underarms on her crutches. "I didn't think you ever walked on the beach."

"Of course I do. It's so good to see you, Malia. What brings you here? And who is your friend?" Bob asked.

"Commodore Bob, this is Mags."

Bob and Mags shook hands.

"Nice to meet you, Mags. That can't be your real name."

"It isn't. It's a shortened version of my name, but it's what everybody calls me."

"Commodore, Mags drove me here because I wanted to see how you are doing and to apologize for the way my parents treated you the other day."

"The first thing we need to do is get you off this sand. Would you like me to carry you?" Bob asked.

"Oh, God, no. I can manage."

They walked on the walkway, crossing the dune to the boardwalk. The three of them sat at the picnic table.

"Malia, no apologies are necessary. Your parents love you very much and they only want what's best for you. They can't make sense out of your pain and their emotions caused them to blame me. I understand completely. Believe me, once you get better, their anger will disappear."

"I hope you're right."

"I'm pretty sure I am, and seeing how fabulous you look, it won't be long before they're back to being their old selves, without the anger. So, tell me, how do you feel? Has any more of your memory returned?"

"Not completely. Every day, I remember more and more, but I can't seem to put the pieces of the puzzle together. My parents refuse to tell me about it, but…"

"Lieutenant Lazecki told me the doctors recommended everyone let your memory come back at its own pace," Bob said.

"I don't think they want me to remember," Malia said.

"You may be right, but they only want what's best for you."

"I actually remember more than I've told them. If I was completely honest with them, I'm afraid they would be angry at how much I already remember. I go back to the doctor on Tuesday. I guess I'll have to come clean with them when I talk to Dr. Williams. I'm really hoping I will remember everything by then."

"Malia, Malia," Bob said. "I would never encourage you to keep anything from your parents. You're pretty smart, right?" Malia smiled, recalling their exchange when they first met. "You'll do what's right. I'm sure of it."

"Well, I can tell you I'm sure whatever happened, happened right here in the dune. I'm also sure it was awful. I keep getting images of Devlin's face and I come back to the fact that you're the reason I'm okay today."

"That's very kind of you to say," Bob said.

"Commodore, I want to stay here talking to you all day, but I promised Mags we would only stay a little while. My parents gave me permission to go with Mags and a few other friends to the Bagel Baker on North Great Neck."

"Oh, I know the Bagel Baker. George makes the best bagels in Virginia Beach, probably anywhere on the east coast outside of New York City."

They stood. Malia hugged Bob so tightly that their respective torso bruises gave each of them a painful reminder they were not yet completely healed.

"When I finally remember everything you did to save

me, I know I'll realize I haven't thanked you enough, Commodore. So, for now, I'll just say thank you and promise I will never forget what you've done," Malia said, nearly on the brink of tears.

"I get it, Malia," Bob said. "You promise never to forget that which you cannot remember. That's priceless!"

The three of them laughed.

"I guess so. That's a pretty awkward way to say it. Isn't it?" Malia said.

"It doesn't matter how you say it. I know it's sincere. Go ahead, ladies. Go meet your friends and enjoy your bagels."

"Commodore Bob, I can't believe I forgot to ask you about Pepper. Where is my little buddy?"

"Oh, he's upstairs doing what dogs do during the day. I'll tell him you were asking for him."

At Bob's suggestion, the girls avoided the sand by walking across the pool deck and the Bay Ridge Condos parking lot to return to Mags' car.

Bob watched as they walked away. They exchanged waves when Malia and Mags looked back before exiting the pool deck.

"He's really something special, isn't he?" Mags said. "Thanks for letting me meet him."

"Thanks for the ride, my friend," Malia said.

When they reached the sidewalk on Page Avenue, they turned right. Malia stopped suddenly and Mags did the same a second later.

"Is that Pepper the dog?" Malia said. She took several steps forward on her crutches and asked Mags to pick up Pepper so she could say hello. Mags had to laugh when she saw the level of enthusiasm in the greetings Malia and Pepper exchanged.

"Hi, Mr. Castalano," Malia said, when she turned her attention from the dog. "I'm surprised to see you walking Pepper for Bob."

"Malia, I'm so sorry. Didn't Lieutenant Lazecki call you?"

"No. Why would he have called me?"

"To tell you...Malia, there's no easy way to say this. Bob died on Friday. Best we can figure is that he went into the dune one more time and it was too much for his heart."

"What are you talking about, Mr. Castalano? My friend Mags and I just saw him."

"Who? The lieutenant?"

"No. The Commodore. We just saw him. We spoke to him. We sat at the picnic table on the boardwalk for a few minutes."

"Malia, you must be mistaken," Tony said.

"No mistake. We saw him. Right, Mags? I hugged him. He hugged me back," Malia said through her tears.

"Malia, are you feeling okay?"

"Sir, Malia introduced me to him. I shook his hand," Mags said.

"Really?" Tony said. "But, of course, you never met Bob before. Have you?"

"What are you saying, Mr. Castalano?" Malia asked. A slight tone of impatience came through in her voice.

"Maybe you saw someone who looked a lot like Bob and made a mistake," Tony said.

"No mistake, Mr. C. We saw him. I may have bumped my head last week, but I am not hallucinating."

Mags nodded to signal her agreement with her friend.

Tony still doubted Malia's story, but he hoped to

change the tone of their conversation by becoming less confrontational.

Malia was clearly convinced she saw Bob, but Tony knew the facts. He was with Bob as he lay dying and he was acutely aware of Malia's injuries. Mags was the unknown factor for Tony. Were it not for Mags, Tony would have concluded Malia was hallucinating.

Mags was either in on a sick joke or Malia convinced herself and her friend that the person they met was Bob Meissner. Tony had no choice but to figure this was a case of mistaken identity.

The person Malia thought was Bob, Tony reasoned, extended the charade either as a joke or because he had ill-intent to these young women. For now though, they were safe.

Tony managed to convince the girls to delay their trip to the Bagel Baker long enough for Malia to say hello to his wife.

As they walked back through the parking lot, Malia formally introduced Tony to Mags.

"How have you been feeling, Malia?" Tony asked her again.

"Mr. Castalano, you've already asked me that question. I'm fine. Honest. I still have bruises, but I haven't had any headaches or dizziness. Really, I'm fine and I know what we saw."

In the Castalano's condo unit, after Tony recapped their meeting for his wife, Mary repeatedly asked Malia about her recovery and what restrictions the doctors put on her.

Her frustration was growing, but Malia tried hard not to let it show.

"Oh, Mrs. Castalano I'm fine. I was not hallucinating. I saw Bob. *We* saw Bob. I don't know what's going on, but I didn't mistake anyone for Bob. It was Bob."

Any tension among them was broken by Pepper who relentlessly tried to get Malia to take a small, cloth chew toy what was shaped like a bird.

"What is this, Pepper? Is this your birdie?" Malia asked, acknowledging that Pepper was not going to stop approaching her with the toy.

"Bob used to call it a parakeet because of its blue and yellow color," Tony said.

Malia repeatedly took the toy from Pepper, who made no effort to play tug-of-war with her. Each time Malia let the toy fall to the carpet, Pepper picked it up and nudged her until she took it again.

"I think he wants you to have it," Mary said.

The few minutes she spent focused on the dog allowed the tension to dissipate between Malia and the Castalanos.

"Mr. and Mrs. Castalano, I admit I'm very confused about all this. I know what happened. It was no illusion. But Mags and I do have to go meet our friends."

"Malia, are you sure you don't want us to give your parents a call to let them know what you say—to let them know what happened to you and Mags?" Mary asked, as she helped Malia stand and handed her the crutches.

"Oh, that's one thing I am most sure of. It's all good. Thank you both, very much," Malia said.

"Honey, come back to visit any time," Mary said. "The three of us would love to see you. Lieutenant Lazecki is working to track down any family Bob might have had. We don't know of any. When we know about a funeral or a memorial service, we'll let you know."

"I wish I had given you my cell number before now."

"We really thought the lieutenant was going to call you or your parents to let you know about Bob."

As the girls walked to the front door, Pepper barked and ran to Malia with the parakeet chew toy in his mouth.

"I promise I will come back to visit, my little friend," she said to the dog.

"Malia," Tony said. "I'm convinced Mary's right. He wants you to have the toy. It's not the newest toy, but, if you don't mind, please take it with you."

Tony picked up the toy and handed it to Malia. Pepper barked once and walked away contentedly.

Malia, Mags, and the Castalanos said their goodbyes.

The truth is incontrovertible.
Malice may attack it,
ignorance may deride it,
but, in the end, there it is.

Winston Churchill

2020 AD

Epilogue

The dune stands. There have been a few big storms, but none so large that the dune was unable to fulfill its protective obligation.

Bo Walsh, Carol's husband, assumed the unofficial title of Protector of the Dune. When people kid him about it, he says he's doing God's work.

Tony and Mary eventually sold their condo. They now live in Florida year-round. Pepper the dog was very much at home in Florida, but died in his sleep after a long life. His spirit is very much alive.

Lieutenant Lazecki declined consideration for promotion to captain. Instead, he submitted his papers and retired at the end of 2010. Before leaving the police force, he handed a box of folders with accounts of unexplained activities in the dune to Detective Sergeant Jake Spires, whose family traces its roots to the original settlers in Virginia Beach. There have been no files added to the box since Bob's death.

Despite his best efforts, Joe Lazecki, now a private citizen, has been unable to identify an elected official willing to pursue any action that might bring increased public attention to the dune.

Malia Matthews graduated from the College of William and Mary and went on to receive a law degree from the University of Virginia. She and her husband live in a suburb of Washington, DC, with their son, Bobby, and their Havanese dog, Pepper.

Resting on Malia's desk, serving as a makeshift paperweight, is the dog toy given to her that Sunday in 2010. When asked, she tells clients it is there to remind her of the spirit of a dear friend.

Nearly every day from spring through fall, dolphins can

be seen at the southern end of the Chesapeake Bay. Just the other day, Bo noticed their pace seemed a bit more hurried than usual, as if they were moving to stay ahead of a storm.

Bo spotted another pod, farther out in the Bay.

"Can you see them?" he called to his wife. "They're way out there, not far from that coaler. Wait! What the hell is a coaler doing there in the Bay?"

Carol came to the balcony carrying binoculars, but the dolphins were already out of sight.

"I can't see any dolphins and I certainly don't see any coaler, either," she said.

In the distance, there was a prolonged, low rumble of thunder.

"Now, I heard and felt that thunder," Carol said.

"Must be a storm coming from somewhere," Bo responded.

"Maybe, but I don't see any rain clouds anywhere."

"Trust me," Bo said. "There's a storm coming."

Bo looked out over the dune and into the Bay. The water was calm. "Behave yourself, Bay. I'll see you tomorrow," Bo said aloud. He turned and went inside.

Soon thereafter, the sun set behind the southern-most span of the Chesapeake Bay Bridge-Tunnel, bringing evening to the community of Bay Ridge Condominiums. And as it did, unseen somewhere in the tall grass, a small opening appeared in the dune.

Acknowledgments

The overwhelmingly positive response to my first novel, *Murder Gets Even*, encouraged me to complete *Death in the Dune* and make it available for you to read. I am grateful most especially to my wife, Eileen. She has willingly assumed the roles of beta reader, editor of first drafts, and loving critic.

My thanks once again extend to Kathy Garvey who, despite her protestation that she is not a proficient editor of fiction, has come through in magnificent fashion. As with *Murder Gets Even*, Kathy's talents extended to the design of the cover for *Death in the Dune*. I cannot overstate my gratitude.

Made in the
USA
Middletown, DE